OJ's MOON

Untold True Stories
from the Other Side

B. T. WEDEMEYER

Dedicated to all those who believed in me.

Contents

CHAPTER 1 — DATE NIGHT

It is Friday, Sept. 8, 1995 in Hollywood, Calif. Michael Nigg is on a late-night dinner date with his beautiful girlfriend, Julie Long. They are traveling south on La Brea Avenue in Julie's new, gold Mercedes Benz sedan, trying to decide on where to eat. Michael is driving. It is a gorgeous evening with temperatures hovering just above 60 degrees.

About eight miles southeast at Los Angeles County Superior Court, the *People vs. O.J. Simpson* murder trial is on recess for the weekend. Simpson, one of the greatest running backs in NFL history, later turned actor and sports broadcaster, is isolated in a 9-by-7-foot cell on the second floor of the county jail in what deputies call the "High Power Unit." This is the place where celebrities, along with serial killers, snitches and dirty cops, are separate from the jail's general population.

Simpson, the NFL Hall-of-Famer and former Heisman Trophy Winner — the man who turned Hertz into the "Superstar of Rent-a-Car" - now simply goes by his booking number:

4013970.

After eight months of grueling courtroom drama, observed by 150 million TV viewers worldwide, the often-dubbed "Trial of the Century" is nearing its dramatic conclusion. Today's big story in the LA Times points out that Simpson's "Dream Team" of defense lawyers has called its last witness, and O.J. will not be taking the stand. Lead attorney Johnnie Cochran and company will spend the weekend planning their next move after a state appellate court overturned an important decision by Judge Lance Ito regarding a racist, dishonest detective named Mark Furhman.

The memorable closing arguments from Cochran and prosecutor Marcia Clark are right around the corner, and a verdict – yes, that verdict – is coming in less than a month.

Like the rest of the world during this time, Michael undoubtedly is aware of what is happening at the Simpson trial up the street. On this evening, however, Julie most certainly has his undivided attention.

A 26-year-old native of Gunnison, Colo., Michael moved to sunny Southern California a few years earlier with dreams of becoming an actor. He has a great smile, and a charming, upbeat personality. He enjoys helping others in need, and he loves to make people laugh.

Like so many other Hollywood dreamers waiting for a chance at stardom, Michael works as a waiter to pay the bills. The Sanctuary, an upscale Beverly Hills restaurant where *Baywatch* bombshell Pamela Anderson met Motley Crue drummer Tommy Lee for the first time, is Michael's current employer. Michael has been off work for a few months with a foot injury, but he is set to return in about a week.

Michael pulls into a Bank of America branch on La Brea hoping to withdraw some cash. The ready teller is closed, however, so Michael goes across the street to Home Savings of America and pulls $40 from an ATM. It is about 10:20 p.m.

The loving couple decides to eat at the El Coyote Café at 7312 Beverly Boulevard in the Fairfax District. The iconic El Coyote is not your typical Mexican diner. For years, the restaurant has attracted Hollywood's biggest stars, including John Wayne, Tony Curtis, Shirley Temple, Jane Fonda and Harrison Ford. Actress/model Sharon Tate and her friends had their last meal here before encountering the Manson family a few hours later at her home on Aug. 9, 1969 – when Michael was 3 months old.

Is tonight the night when Michael strikes gold and catches his lucky break – a chance encounter with a Hollywood executive who can get his non-injured foot through the front door, or is he thinking about something a little less life altering, such as washing down a delicious Enchilada Howard with one of El Coyote's legendary margaritas?

After Michael turns onto Beverly Boulevard, his first mission is to find parking, which is no easy task in this busy commercial district on a Friday night. He turns north on Poinsettia Place, a residential street about a half-block from the restaurant, and immediately spots an unattended parking lot to his left behind The Art Store. To get to the restaurant, the couple will just have to take a short walk back to Beverly and cross the boulevard.

As they turn into the small parking lot, Michael and Julie have no reason to notice a white sedan parked next to the curb across the street with its lights off. Three male occupants are inside.

On this date, the No. 1 song on the Billboard Charts is "Gangsta's Paradise," a song by a rap artist known as Coolio.

Michael parks between two other vehicles and secures the steering wheel with an anti-theft device known as The Club. He opens his door and Julie immediately hears another man's voice coming from the direction of Poinsettia Place.

"Hey man!"

"HEY MAN!"

Michael is standing just inside the driver's side door when he turns towards the rear of the car. Julie, who is still inside the vehicle, hears that same voice again.

"Give me all your money!"

Still seated in the car, Julie can now see that Michael is standing face-to-face with an adult Black male. Suddenly, there is a scuffle and, without warning, a loud bang.

Everything is happening so fast. Julie is obviously frightened and confused. As she reaches for her cell phone, she sees not one, but two, adult Black males running away from the parking lot and north on Poinsettia Place into the residential neighborhood. Julie gets out of the car and runs around to the driver's side, where she finds her one true love lying in blood. She begins screaming for help.

As this horrific event is unfolding, the suspects do not realize that five women are sitting in a parked Izuzu Trooper in the next aisle over. Carina Longworth, Lesley Mobbs, Dana Bilvado, Lisa Schipper and April Reynolds, all in their late 20s and early 30s, have just finished walking back to the vehicle after dining at El Coyote. Longworth is backing out of the parking space when Mobbs notices an adult Black male approaching from the street.

"Lock the doors!" Mobbs yells.

The man seems to hear Mobbs and ducks out of sight. Longworth continues backing out of the parking space before noticing a Black male standing a short distance away beyond the front of her vehicle. Seconds later, she hears a gunshot followed by a woman's screams. As she peels out of the parking lot, Longworth sees a woman standing next to her car holding a cell phone. At the intersection of Poinsettia and Beverly, she pulls into a lighted parking lot at Kearns Market, where two of her friends call 911.

Meanwhile, 30-year-old Jennifer Lane, and Susan Westcott, 32, have also just finished eating at El Coyote, and are walking back to the same lot where Michael and Julie parked. They round the corner at The Art Store and proceed north on Poinsettia before Lane notices a Black male approaching in the opposite direction about 15 feet away. The man appears to be holding an object in his right hand.

At that moment, Lane hears a loud noise coming from the parking lot, which is just out of her view behind The Art Store. The women then observe two Black males walking quickly out of the parking lot before proceeding north on Poinsettia. Lane and Westcott continue towards the parking lot and observe a woman standing next to her Mercedes screaming.

"Help me! Someone just shot my boyfriend!"

After seeing the young man on the pavement, Westcott runs over attempts CPR. She is unable to clear his airway.

Esther Adler, 59, who lives just a few houses north of the parking lot at 330 N. Poinsettia Place, is in her upstairs bedroom when she hears a loud gunshot followed by screams. She looks out her window and notices an unfamiliar white sedan with a sunroof in front of her next-door neighbor's home. She then witnesses two adult Black males running across the street from the parking lot towards the vehicle. One of the men pauses at the driver's side door before getting in the back seat. The other man gets into the right front passenger seat. Before he could even close the door, the car takes off north on Poinsettia Place towards Oakwood Avenue. Adler calls 911.

Howard Ratzky, 56, is walking his dog on Oakwood near Poinsettia Place when he hears a gunshot in the distance, followed by a woman's screams. About 60 seconds later, he observes a white sedan coming north on Poinsettia Place. After turning east on Oakwood, the vehicle passes Ratzky, who notices a Black male roughly 30 years of age in the right front passenger seat.

Two uniformed LAPD officers, L. Perez and M. Pedroza, are the first to arrive at the crime scene at 10:49 p.m. Moments later, a Los Angeles City Fire Department rescue ambulance pulls up as the officers call in for additional units to establish a perimeter.

Michael is transported to Cedars-Sinai Medical Center, where he is pronounced dead at 11:17 p.m. His murder is one of 1,682 homicides in Los Angeles County in 1995 – one of the deadliest years in the county's history. Nearly half of these homicides are gang-related. Hundreds of others are robberies just like Michael's unsolved case.

Back at the crime scene, another first responder, identified as Officer Bowman, is looking around for clues. He notices a tan purse with a shoulder strap lying on the roadway just in front of The Art Store. He figures the purse probably belongs to Julie, so he picks it up and hands it over to one of the homicide detectives.

When investigators find no money on Michael, they assume these robbers got away with the $40 he pulled from the ATM. However, when Michael's best friend and roommate, Robbie Suelett, pulls Julie's Mercedes out of inpound at Hollywood Tow several days later, they find Michael's wallet in his satchel on the back seat. Inside are two crisp $20 bills. In return for this cold, senseless and cowardly murder, the armed robbers get nothing.

Around the time of Michael's death, LAPD is struggling to keep pace with the growing number of robbery-homicides due to an unpopular reorganization by Police Chief Willie L. Williams earlier in the year. LAPD has a team assigned to investigating officer-involved shootings. When District Attorney Gil Garcetti complains that the team is more interested in protecting fellow officers, Williams turns over all police-involved shootings to the Robbery-Homicide Division, which boasts 36 of LAPD's best homicide detectives. Many of the shootings do not even involve a victim.

Meanwhile, over a seven-month period in 1995, the Robbery-Homicide Division takes on only four new robbery-homicide cases. Dozens of other murder cases are distributed among city's geographical police divisions, which already have their own busy caseload with new homicides happening every day.

Robbery-Homicide detectives, who just want to do their jobs, send a letter to Chief Williams expressing their frustration, prompting an article in the Dec. 5, 1995 issue of the Los Angeles Times.

"We hope you will . . . see the waste of talent, expertise and resources that the RHD reorganization has caused." Two of the many detectives who sign the letter just happen to be Philip Vannatter and Tom Lange, lead investigators in the Simpson case.

A detective named Richard Jackson is the primary author of the letter.

"To be blunt, we are wasting our expertise," Jackson writes.

Normally, Michael's murder would not attract huge media attention, especially if it is buried under a pile of other cases on a busy detective's desk. Michael, who appeared on one episode of a syndicated TV game show called "Liars," has not reached celebrity status. He is not a professional athlete, singer, politician or rapper. Tragically, this kind of thing happens every night in Los Angeles. It is just not that newsworthy in the eyes of media.

However, as they say, it is not what you know, it is *who* you know.

Over the weekend following Michael's death, the media, frantically searching for any stories that have some Juice, learn something interesting about a homicide victim in Hollywood that Friday night. It turns out that Michael was once a friend and co-worker of another unsolved murder victim, and this victim is on the minds of millions of people across the globe. Before taking the job at The Sanctuary, Michael worked at a popular Italian eatery in Brentwood known as the Mezzaluna.

On Sept. 12, 1995, four days after Michael's death, a 222-word story comes across the Associated Press wire. The headline reads, "Friend of Ronald Goldman Fatally Shot by Thieves."

CHAPTER 2 – DOUBT

It is the afternoon of Friday, March 26, 2021, in a quiet mobile home park in Parker, Ariz. I live here in a three-bedroom manufactured home with my girlfriend, along with two teenagers, three little dogs, a cat, a snake and some tiny fish.

I just returned home from work as principal of Le Pera Elementary School, a small K-8 school on the Colorado River Indian Tribes reservation about 20 miles south of here. The tribes lease the school property to the Parker Unified School District so we can provide an education to about 200 children, many of them living in poverty on the reservation. I decide to knock out some chores before my girlfriend comes home from her job as a dispatch supervisor.

We live a short walking distance from the Colorado River, which serves as the border between Arizona and California. Directly across the river is Earp, Calif., an unincorporated community named after the famous Old West legend, Wyatt Earp, who mined for copper and gold in the nearby Whipple Mountains during the sunset of his life. Lake Havasu City, Ariz., a popular Spring Break destination and home to the world famous London Bridge, is 40 miles upriver. Blythe, Calif., a dusty desert stop along Interstate 10, is 50 miles downriver.

With a population of about 3,200, Parker is at the center of the hottest region in the country, often showing up dark red on most TV weather maps during the summer months. It is common for temperatures to exceed 120 degrees in these parts in July or August. On this day, however, summer is just knocking on the door with a high of 74 degrees. Next Friday, the high will be 97 degrees.

This is my eighth year as principal of this wonderful school after teaching high school and middle school English for seven. However, while I love helping kids discover their potential, education is not my *first* love. I am really a journalist at heart.

After spending four years in the Air Force as a photojournalist, including a short tour in Operation Desert Storm, I worked 15 more years in the civilian world as a small newspaper reporter and editor. I started a career in education in the early 2000s because I thought I needed a change. I wanted to coach baseball. Call it an early mid-life crisis after my first divorce.

Gathering the news and "scooping" the competition is still in my blood. To this day, I often sit at my desk and second-guess that decision to change careers. I sometimes dream about packing up and walking back into a small town paper somewhere – anywhere – and offering my services as an old school news hound who can work the phones, develop sources, ask tough questions, get good quotes and write catchy leads. Nothing gets your blood pumping like knowing there is 45 minutes until deadline, and you still owe your editor 12 inches of copy. Man, I miss those days.

Then I wonder if American journalism, with its steady transformation into this fast-paced digital world, really still has a place for a middle-aged school principal who hasn't seen a byline since 2005. I have a Facebook page, and that's about it. I do not Tweet. I do not Instagram. I do not Tik Tok. Heck, when I started in journalism, newspapers were still developing their own film and using electric typewriters. Today, people get their news off their phones instead of their driveways.

It looks like I will continue watching students laugh and learn while my teachers adapt and overcome every possible obstacle. I have an important and fulfilling career. The pay is good. Life is good. This is who I am — a school administrator who *used* to write the news for a living.

I guess I should learn never to get too comfortable.

As I fold some laundry in my bedroom, I am casually streaming a documentary on what is arguably the most talked-about murder case in American history. The filmmakers are exploring whether or not somebody *else* killed Nicole Brown Simpson and Ronald Goldman on the night of June 12, 1994 at 875 S. Bundy Drive in Brentwood, Calif.

Before I continue, I should note that I am extremely skeptical when it comes to conspiracy theories. I consider most of them to be tunnel-focused, using so-called evidence that only supports an alleged conspiracy while ignoring other contradictory facts that point directly to the, dare I say . . . *truth?*

For example, I have a friend who insists that a missile struck the Pentagon on 9/11 – and not a passenger jet. He can talk for hours trying to prove his case that our government attacked its own military headquarters, but when I ask him how he might explain his theory to the grieving families of the 64 passengers of American Airlines Flight 77 - and maybe offer a suggestion on where they might be located — he loses steam quickly.

Conspiracy theories can hurt people - good people who are just trying to get on with their lives. It is one thing to toss around whodunits on a big murder case in your own backyard, as I will do often over the next three years of my life. It is quite another to start spitting out theories that have nothing to do with truth on social media, and then regurgitating them, over and over and over again.

Ask Alex Jones, the wacky conspiracy theorist who is required to pay more than $1.1 billion in civil damages to the grieving families of the Sandy Hook Elementary School massacre in 2012. Jones tried to convince anyone who would listen that the deadliest school shooting in American history was a hoax.

Yet, while I consider myself cautious when it comes to conspiracy theories, I must admit that my own personal feelings about the O.J. Simpson case have always been rooted in doubt – reasonable or otherwise.

I was just 25 years old when O.J. Simpson declared himself "absolutely, 100-percent not guilty" to the double-murder charges during his arraignment on June 22, 1994. In fact, Ronald Goldman and I were born just about six weeks apart.

During the "Trial of the Century," I worked as the sports editor of a weekly newspaper in Clovis, Calif. We had a small, black-and-white television in our newsroom located in the corner of the ceiling just above my desk. The trial had priority over all other programming for the next eight months – even San Francisco Giants games.

Like so many other Americans, I could not turn away from the courtroom drama. My boss had to remind me more than a few times that the sports section was not going to produce itself. When there was a big moment during the trial, and co-workers would start hovering around my desk, I always felt it was my responsibility to bring them up to speed on the latest developments. I was their built-in TV commentator, live and in-person.

The popular opinion among those in the office – made up almost entirely of middle class Caucasian folks from this little cowboy town in California's heartland — was that Simpson was guilty as sin. I was the lone wolf in the room. While I agreed — at the time — that the evidence against O.J. was significant, I also believed there was enough for the jury to have reasonable doubt. I debated often with my co-workers, and when I predicted an acquittal, they shoved me aside as being young and naïve. They were mostly right. At that age, my priorities were draft beer, fast food and slow-pitch softball.

I will always remember the level of shock and disgust in that newsroom when the jury reached its verdict on Oct. 3, 1995. I am sure I looked silly doing a celebration dance around the newsroom as if I just caught a touchdown pass from Niners quarterback Steve Young. It was not so much that I cared about O.J.'s guilt or innocence. This annoying brat was just happy about being right, and I had no problem rubbing it in while I collected my winnings on a $20 bet with the advertising manager.

Young and naïve? Probably. Immature? Absolutely.

For me, the "Trial of the Century" was nothing more than a fun TV show. For one of my co-workers — a divorced single mom and a victim of domestic violence herself — the trial was something much more personal. My childish celebration tempered quickly when I saw her quietly wipe tears from her face and return to her desk.

I should have known better. I remember her coming into the office with a black eye on more than one occasion. I remember seeing her cry while her husband was screaming at her over the telephone. I am sure in her heart she genuinely believed O.J. was guilty. She listened to that recording of the 911 call, and she understood the fear that Nicole had to live with. She probably also appreciated Nicole's disappointment with law enforcement.

"You guys have been up here eight times before, all you do is talk to him, you never do anything," Nicole told an emergency dispatcher during one of those famous 911 calls. "He's gonna kill me."

For that co-worker, I am sure a guilty verdict would have served as a small victory against domestic violence. Instead, in her eyes, Simpson was just another example of an abusive spouse getting away with murder – both figuratively and literally.

At that time, the American justice system was just learning how to deal with domestic violence. Two months after the murders of Ron and Nicole, President Bill Clinton signed the Violence Against Women Act of 1994. Democratic Senator Joe Biden, in what is widely regarded as one of his greatest political achievements to this day, sponsored the bill providing $1.6 billion toward investigation and prosecution of violent crimes against women

I am 55 years old now, and I would like to think I am a little wiser to the world. I wish I could find that co-worker so

I could apologize for my childish and insensitive behavior that day.

Still, after all that, my opinion about the case has not really altered. In fact, I am convinced more than ever that those jurors reached the correct conclusion almost three decades ago. There was plenty of reasonable doubt at their fingertips, and that was only the evidence and testimony they were *allowed* to consider.

I am just a school principal now. I am not thinking about writing even a paragraph – much less an entire book. If somebody told me I would someday be writing a true crime book related to the O.J. Simpson case, I would call them crazy. Since that famous acquittal, I don't think I have discussed the case longer than five minutes with anybody.

Still, even though I think it is likely that O.J. is responsible for the murders, a small portion of doubt still lingers within me to this day. Maybe this mindset is what prompts me to watch a documentary like this. If I am actually open to the possibility that O.J. is innocent, then I have to be open to the possibility that somebody else killed Ron and Nicole. Don't I? Maybe these folks on television offer a plausible theory of some sort.

As I fold up my Phoenix Suns T-shirt, the documentarians are rehashing the so-called timeline of events on the night of June 12, 1994. The prosecution's timeline was always a huge issue for me. I just have a hard time believing that O.J. had enough opportunity to do *everything* he is accused of before hopping on a plane to Chicago.

I am even more skeptical about another timeline that is less talked about over the years since the murders. Does Ronald Goldman really have enough time to clock out from his job as a waiter, chat at the bar with his co-workers, walk home, eat something, shower, change and *drive* to Nicole's condo when the prosecution says he does? In 20 minutes? At this particular moment, before my journey begins, it is something that I just cannot wrap my head around.

As I ponder over these details, a question suddenly pops into my head that will ultimately turn my entire world upside down and awaken that small-time investigative journalist you never heard of still inside me.

The question is . . .

How did Ron get to Nicole's house?

CHAPTER 3 – THE QUESTION

We all know about the white Ford Bronco. It is arguably the most famous vehicle ever seen on television – even more popular than "General Lee" on *The Dukes of Hazzard.* About 95 million people, including myself, watched the slow-speed chase along Interstate 405 on June 17, 1994 — many of us wondering if O.J. Simpson was about to take his own life at any moment. If you believe what many people do, a white Ford Bronco is also what transported a celebrity murderer to and from the gruesome crime scene at 875 South Bundy Drive earlier in the week.

However, I cannot help thinking to myself – shouldn't Ron's method of transportation also have at least *some* significance in this case? After all the time I spent watching the trial, not to mention all the documentaries and news coverage that follow, why is my mind drawing a complete blank on this subject?

Before I continue, I think it's important to offer a quick recount of the somewhat established timeline of events that take place on the night of June 12, 1994. One thing I learn quickly during this journey is that most people I talk to about the case either don't remember the story of that night, or they are just too young to remember. It is hard to believe that three decades have already gone by.

After both O.J. and Nicole, who are not getting along very well at this time, attend a dance recital for their daughter in the afternoon, Nicole and her family go to dinner at the Mezzaluna Restaurant, which is walking distance from her home in Brentwood. O.J. is not invited. They leave the restaurant at about 8 p.m. Here is what we know happened after that:

9:33 p.m. – Ron Goldman, a waiter who is also friends with Nicole, clocks out at the Mezzaluna Restaurant.

9:37 p.m. – Nicole's mother, Juditha Brown, calls the Mezzaluna to say she lost her eyeglasses.

9:40 p.m. – O.J. and his guest house resident, Kato Kaelin, return home from a drive-thru run at McDonald's. Juditha calls Nicole about the glasses.

9:45 p.m. – Nicole calls the Mezzaluna and talks to both Karen Crawford and Ron Goldman.

9:50-9:55 p.m. – Ron leaves the Mezzaluna.

10:15 p.m. – A neighbor across the alley behind Nicole's condo begins to hear constant loud barking. Prosecutor Marcia Clark later tells a jury this must be when the double-homicide takes place.

10:25 p.m. – Limousine Driver Alan Park arrives at Simpson's home to take him to the airport.

10:40 p.m. – Kaelin hears three loud thumps

on the wall from just outside the guest house. Robert Heidstra, who is walking his small dogs in an alley directly across the street from Nicole's condo, hears a young man yell "Hey, Hey, Hey!"

10:40-10:50 p.m. – Park buzzes Simpson's intercom several times with no answer.

10:55 p.m. – Park calls his boss to say Simpson is not home. Boss tells him to wait until 11:15 p.m.

Just before 11 p.m. – Park sees a Black male, about 6 feet tall and 200 pounds, walking towards Simpson's home.

11 p.m. – Kaelin goes to the front of the house to check on the noise. Park buzzes the intercom again and Simpson answers. Simpson tells Park that he overslept, and he is in the shower.

11:15 p.m. – Park and Simpson take off in the limousine for LAX.

11:45 p.m. – Simpson's American Airlines flight departs for the Chicago.

12:10 a.m. – The bodies of Nicole and Ron are discovered outside her condo at 875 South Bundy Drive.

So there it is. There is not much dispute over the major stamps on this timeline. However, there is plenty of discussion and debate over what happens everywhere in between, especially during the time in which O.J. is unaccounted for between roughly 9:45 and 11 p.m.

The popular narrative for Ron Goldman on this night is "wrong place at the wrong time." Although many conspiracy theorists will suggest otherwise, Ron, as you may recall, is doing a friend a favor. Nicole's mom accidentally dropped her eyeglasses at the Mezzaluna earlier that evening. Ron is simply returning them to her daughter, Nicole, on his way to meet some friends at a club in Santa Monica. That is the story.

However, I have never stopped to think about *how* Ron gets to Nicole's condo. Wouldn't his car, or truck, or motorcycle for that matter, be parked right out front? Heck, Ron could have left the engine running, potentially offering more clarity within this extremely tight timeline.

Ron's vehicle must have at least some value during the murder investigation. Where does Ron park? How do police learn which vehicle nearby belongs to him? When do they find out? Do police detectives thoroughly search the vehicle for clues? Do they find any drugs, or weapons, or maybe even blood? Do they dust the vehicle for fingerprints? Do they give Ron's vehicle the same tender-loving investigative care (I use that term loosely) they offer the Bronco? If not, why not? If so, what do they find? How about a receipt from a gas station or a fast-food restaurant? Maybe he stops somewhere before arriving at Nicole's.

As these questions enter my mind, unfortunately the conspiracy theorist in me is now rearing its ugly head. If Ron's vehicle is not considered relevant to the investigation, do police miss something? Is it impossible to believe that Ron is not alone on his way to Nicole's residence? Is it impossible to believe that Ron is actually under some sort of duress long before he gets there? Maybe Ron already knows there is a situation brewing at Nicole's? Maybe the contents of his vehicle offer clues to a double murder that has nothing to do with O.J.'s so-called raging jealousy, and everything to do with Ron somehow?

The next morning, I take these unanswered questions to work with me in my head. It is a Saturday, and I need to finish up on some teacher evaluations — one of the not-so-fun aspects of being a school administrator.

After I am done with the important stuff that pays the bills, I grab a Diet Pepsi from the teacher's lounge, sit back down at my computer, and start to Google. My mission: find out how Ron got to Nicole's house. Get the question out of my system and move on with my life. I have enough other things to keep me distracted. Did I mention I have a severe case of ADHD?

I have always considered myself a competent Google searcher . . . if that means anything. When there is a friendly debate about another role an actor has played on television, or what old-school jam is being sampled on Top 40 radio, or who played third base for the Cincinnati Reds in 1990 (Chris Sabo hit 38 doubles that year), I am usually the person who whips out the cell phone and finds the quick answer. How did Ron get to Nicole's condo? No problem. I got this.

Well, now it is four hours later, and I am still looking. Nothing. I just cannot believe I have not found a specific answer by now. When I Google "How did Ron Goldman get to Nicole's house?" there are more than 2 million links offered. Yet, link after link on Google page after Google page, I cannot find anything. Of course, that only makes me more curious, and honestly, even a little bit suspicious.

Maybe I am looking in the wrong direction. At my school, we teach the difference between secondary sources and primary sources as early as 3rd grade. Even though many are filled with all sorts of interesting tidbits, all of these Google hits are giving me secondary sources with other interests and story angles in mind. As a result, Ron's vehicle becomes inconsequential. With this many links on the web, it appears I am likely looking for a needle in a haystack.

However, now I really need to know. I call my fiancé and tell her I will be a few hours late. I can feel myself at the early stages of obsession. Maybe I can find something on the Internet in terms of *primary* sources. In other words, maybe it is time to start reading actual court transcripts and other first-hand, official documents from the OJ trial. Some of them have to be out there somewhere. Search: "OJ trial transcripts."

The very first link at the top of my Google search reads "Jack Walraven's Simpson Trial Transcripts." Sounds promising, and . . . click. I scan down the page and find links for everything I can imagine, and more. It is not one primary source. It is a smorgasbord of primary sources, including transcripts from both the criminal and civil trials, preliminary hearings, grand jury testimony, motions, court orders, depositions, juror lists and interviews, evidence lists, on and on.

Jack Walraven, who grew up in the Netherlands before emigrating to British Columbia, actually started creating this archive way back in 1994 while the criminal trial was underway.

"At the time, the World Wide Web was in its infancy and I was just getting my feet wet on the Internet," Walraven writes on his site. "Collecting the transcripts and making them publicly available seemed like an interesting exercise."

At the top of the web page, there is also a link to a New

York Times article from Feb. 14, 1995 – in which Walraven and others talk about how the young Internet has emerged as a "global repository" of trial news, trivia and discussion.

"We are as up to date as the lawyers themselves are," Walraven boasts. "Because we have access to all the information, it makes for intelligent discussions."

Dank u meneer Walraven!

At this moment, I have forgotten about Ron Goldman's vehicle. I feel like a kid again walking into Disneyland for the first time. I cannot wait to go on the first ride, but where do I start? It is a problem I do not mind having. I decide it will be more fun to go on a ride that is new to me.

The civil trial.

In 1996, Ron's parents, Fred Goldman and Sharon Rufo, along with Nicole Simpson's father, Lou Brown, filed a wrongful death lawsuit against O.J. before a judge eventually awarded the families $33.5 million in damages. It was a major victory for those who believed – as many still do – that the jury in the criminal trial blew its chance to hold O.J. accountable.

I decide to dig into the pre-trial witness depositions first. Depositions are a time for discovery, and much of what happens here will never get addressed in the actual trial. I do not want to miss any mentions of Ron's vehicle, so this is where I will start.

During one of these depositions, attorney Daniel Petrocelli, representing the Goldman family, kindly reminds folks in the room that "Mezzaluna" stands for crescent moon in Italian. This translation really sticks with me and, in my mind, becomes the perfect metaphor for everything I am doing. In science class, we learn that the moon makes a full spin on its axis in the same amount of time it takes to the orbit the Earth – every 27.3 days. One web site I find compares it to a race car that drifts as it moves around a slippery dirt track, constantly pointing its front bumper to the center. The first time humans actually see the other side of the moon is in 1959 through images from a Soviet spacecraft.

Likewise, humans all over the world seem to look at the "Trial of the Century" with one particular lens, which is "Did he do it?" There is plenty to talk about on this bright side, but I will soon come to learn that the other side of O.J.'s Moon offers several bizarre twists and turns with new storylines, new characters and sadly, even more tragedy.

There are 31 total days of depositions during nearly a six-month period in the first half of 1996, including the first nine days spent with O.J. himself. I figure O.J. probably does not have much to say about Ron's travel patterns, so I decide to skip him for now. I would also just like to hear from somebody new for a change.

The next witness to give a deposition is a woman named Cora Fischman. Her testimony takes three days starting on March 19, 1996. I am not familiar with this name. Perfect.

Before I start reading, I do a quick Google search on Fischman and learn she was a close, personal friend of Nicole. I also notice an Associated Press article with a juicy headline that reads, "Friend Says Victim's Final Weeks Marked by Sex, Possible Drug Use." I remind myself that I am going to rely on primary sources whenever possible, so I hold off reading the article and go directly to the transcript.

Sex and drugs? Now we are talking. I do not recall sex and drugs being a main focus of the criminal trial, and I did not follow the civil trial with any fervor whatsoever, so I am excited about what I might learn from this Fischman lady.

However, I soon realize this is not going to be an easy, casual read. The word count from the transcript on just the first day of Fischman's deposition is 47,607. Some entire novels are published in less. When I cut and paste it on to a word document, it takes up 251 pages. So, instead of attempting to tackle this beast word for word, I decide to slowly scan my way down looking for any mentions of Ron Goldman and his vehicle. I will also just go ahead and keep my eyes open for sex and drugs. Why not?

Petrocelli is questioning Cora Fischman about a wide variety of topics. Her pending lawsuit against the National Enquirer, her media interviews after the murders, her potential book deals, her divorce.

And Faye Resnick. I do recall Faye Resnick as another one of Nicole's best friends. I also remember her creating a storm during the criminal trial when she published the book, "*Nicole Brown Simpson: The Private Diary of a Life Interrupted.*"

Petrocelli asks Fischman if anybody besides O.J. Simpson entered her mind as the possible killer in the days following the murders. She responds, "At the time, yes."

Now . . . we're talking.

Q: Who?

A: — because, see, Faye Resnick — see, Faye Resnick was running out of money; she didn't have a home, and they were doing a lot of — they were doing cocaine and they were doing — they were soliciting men, and so they were out almost every night, and so I said, "Oh, my God, somebody could have done" — you know.

Hold up. Pause. Pause. Pause. Let me get this straight. According to this woman, Fischman - a close friend - Faye Resnick and Nicole are doing coke, soliciting men and in

31

need of money? Just days before the murders? For this casual follower of the O.J. trial nearly three decades ago, this is somewhat of an "aha" moment for me. I recall some theories about Columbian drug lords, but it seemed like a reach for me at the time. It apparently is a reach for Judge Lance Ito during the criminal trial as well, as he does not allow the jury to hear testimony about Resnick's drug use. He says there is no evidence connecting cocaine to the murders.

I notice Faye Resnick is on the list of witnesses who gave depositions in the civil trial. I decide to click on her name and see if she has anything to say under oath about drug use. Sure enough, Resnick explains how she goes into treatment for cocaine addiction in 1992 after her sister dies and her father goes into a coma. She is also going through a divorce at the time. She remains sober until relapsing just a few weeks before the murders.

Q: What quantity of cocaine were you taking when you relapsed in June of 1994?

A. I used to do $20 a day when I would do cocaine.

Q. What kind, what quantity of cocaine did $20 buy?

A. A quarter of a gram.

Q. What was the total dollar amount of cocaine that you used during this relapse in June 1994, until you went into the treatment center?

A. I think, at most, $200.

On June 9, 1994 – three days before the murders, Faye Resnick goes into rehab at the Exodus Treatment Center in Los Angeles. On June 12, at 9 p.m., less than two hours before the murders, she calls Nicole from the rehab center. Petrocelli asks her what she discussed with Nicole.

A: "I asked her how the recital went and she said it was great. She focused on the kids the most, and the recital, the conversation regarding the recital. I asked her if she - if O.J. showed up and she said she did - he did. I asked her how she, what did she say to him and she said she told him to leave her alone, that he was not wel-come in her family any longer, that he was not welcome to join them for dinner. She said he was in a deep, dark mood and she said that he had been trying to get a hold of her and she wasn't returning his phone calls, or that she wasn't talking to him. And she was - the rest of the conversation was just brilliant. She was just the happiest girl I had ever talked to. She was free. She said she was free. And she was. She was free of him for a very short period of time."

My first day of searching for Ron's method of travel on the night of June 12, 1994 proves unsuccessful. However, I enjoy learning all this *new* information about the case. New to me, anyways. I return home, and my fiancé is waiting for me in the backyard with an ice-cold beer. We definitely have a fun topic of conversation for tonight.

At this stage of my journey, my fiancé and I agree with the jury's "not guilty" verdict in the criminal trial. We believe there *is* room for reasonable doubt, and since that is the case, and we are at least open to the possibility that O.J. is innocent, we have to be open to other possible scenarios that night that do not involve the Juice.

Armed with our new information about sex, drugs and Ron's still missing vehicle, not to mention an 18-pack of Coors Light, we begin to start developing scenarios that I am sure would make the Goldman and Brown families cringe.

Hey, at least we are in the privacy of our own home and not producing a podcast for the masses.

My fiancé is a little more street smart than I am. She starts painting a picture in which Ron Goldman – not Nicole – is the potential primary target in this double homicide. She offers a hypothetical in which Ron shows up at Nicole's to, let's just say, conduct some business and make a little cash on his way to the club. Maybe the story about her mom's glasses is just a front. I start to chime in with what I have learned so far. Maybe Nicole's emotional telephone conversation with Faye Resnick is more about fear. Maybe Faye's suppliers are following Ron, and when they learn there is no money to collect, or even worse, that Faye Resnick will be gone for an extended period, they are not happy. Maybe they are afraid that Faye is going to turn snitch.

As we go round and round, we become more and more open to the idea that these murders *might* have something to do with the "C" word – cocaine. This was the early 90s in the most affluent part of Southern California. Nicole's circle of friends, including Faye and Ron, liked to club hop until the wee hours. Why is it so hard to believe?

The Goldman family, to this day, insists that Ron was never a drug user, much less a drug dealer. Makes sense. Then again, if I was in the game, I can assure you my father would never know. My sister? Possibly. Father? No way.

I will later find out that Ron, at the time of his murder, is quietly making very extensive plans for his own restaurant/club called "Ankh." While his sister knows all about it, Ron keeps these plans away from his father, Fred Goldman.

". . . Ron was not going to share them with me until he felt they were professional and complete enough to impress me," Fred writes in the book, *His Name is Ron: Our Search for Justice.*

If Ron does not want his dad to know about Ankh until the time is right, he certainly is not going to tell him about coke *if* that is a part of his life.

Then who would know? Well, how about his friends? Many years have gone by since that horrible night. Maybe some of his friends are willing to share what they know about Ron, but how do I find them?

In the news media, we have two jobs to do in the wake of a deadly tragedy. The first is to go out and gather the facts. Who? What? When? Where? Why? and How? Basic Journalism 101. The other is to go out and gather quotes. Talk to friends of the victims. Get some nice quotes. Package them together in a story and send it to the editor.

I did this same thing as a reporter in Lake Havasu City in 2010 after one of the deadliest murder-suicides in Arizona history. A 26-year-old man went to the home of his estranged ex-girlfriend and opened fire during a party, killing five people before driving all the way to California to kill himself. The story made national news. Our crime beat reporter got the facts. I got the quotes about the victims from the people who loved them.

Maybe this is how I can find some of Ron's friends, because the same thing happens in the wake of Ron and Nicole's murders. The Los Angeles Times puts their best people on the facts, while assigning a few others to get quotes about Ron. From the LA Times:

"To pay the rent he worked as a waiter," friend Peter Argyris said in an interview with a local television station. "But he loved teaching kids."

This is one of several *nice* quotes in the article. I mean, nobody with any human decency is going to say something shady or controversial to the press about a friend who is brutally murdered less than two days earlier, right? Peter Argyris would not know anything about Ron and the "C" word, anyways . . . would he?

My fiancé and I continue discuss the O.J. case over the next several days and nights. Meanwhile, I continue to search through the civil trial depositions for sex, drugs, Ron's vehicle . . .

. . . and his friends.

CHAPTER 4 — WHO IS "MIKE?"

I decide to turn my attention on the deposition of Kim Gold-man, Ron's younger sister. Maybe she will reveal some clues in this transcript on what Ron was driving or whom he hung out with at the time. I recall Kim being at her father's side for most of the criminal trial. I remember how visible her pain was in the courtroom after the jury announced its verdict.

After a quick web search, I learn that Kim is now an author and a well-known victim advocate. My mother was a longtime victim advocate for the courts here before she died, so Kim has my immediate respect and admiration. More recently, Kim starts a podcast called "Media Circus," which explores how the media covers high-profile crimes. Her web site reads:

Media Circus connects you with the real people beyond the media coverage to share their stories — in their own words, on their own terms."

I bet Kim Goldman would not appreciate where my mind is at during the early stages of this journey. She obviously does not have much patience for internet conspiracy the-orists who do not have all the facts. While I do not think of myself as such, I guess if I walk like a duck . . .

"I would want people to be a bit more discerning when they're looking at information on the internet," Kim tells Fox News in 2022. "I know it's exhausting to read through 20 different articles to hopefully find the truth. But just be mindful about where you get your information."

This is strong advice that sticks with me throughout this adventure. However, I still have questions, and if there is one source of information that should pass Kim's muster – it is Kim herself. Phil Baker, an attorney for O.J. Simpson, examines Kim during a civil trial deposition on Feb. 5, 1996. Almost immediately, I learn something new from Kim — that her brother, prior to his death, was a partner in a business called "Design Wrap," which puts on big parties for entertainers and such after they finish a movie or a music recording, etc. One of those partners she identifies as a man named Jeffrey Fong. Maybe Mr. Fong is someone I can search for later on. Then Baker's questions take a strange turn.

Q. Have you ever heard the name [Name Deleted]?

A. No.

Q. How about [Name Deleted]?

A. Yes.

To be clear, I am not the one deleting the name from the transcript. That is exactly how it reads. I have seen this before as a news reporter while sifting through police reports, which often exclude the name of a victim or witness to protect their privacy. Let us continue . . .

Q. Where have you heard his name?

A. I met [Name Deleted] in Santa Barbara. And I know he was friends with Ron.

Q. When did you meet him in Santa Barbara?

A. '92, maybe.

Q. How did you meet him?

A. Mutual friends.

Q. Was Ron there?

A. No.

Q. Were you introduced to him randomly, or were you supposed to meet?

A. Blind date.

Q. You and [Name Deleted] were on a blind date?

A. Uh-huh.

THE REPORTER "Yes"?

THE WITNESS: Yes. Sorry.

Q. Did you see him after that night?

A. Yes.

Q. On how many times?

A. A handful.

Q. Is that 5?

A. 5.

Q. Did you go out with him?

A. In a group of people.

Q. You never were dating [Name Deleted]?

A. No.

Q. What did he do for a living?

A. At this time?

Q. Yes.

A. He worked at – I always forget the name – at a restaurant in Santa Barbara.

MR. PETROCELLI: What's the time frame?

MR. P. BAKER:

Q. 1992 he worked at a restaurant in Santa Barbara?

A. Yes.

Q. Do you remember the name of the restaurant?

A. No.

Q. Do you know what he did following his work at the Santa Barbara restaurant?

A. He moved to Los Angeles.

Q. Did you ever see him in Los Angeles?

A. No.

Q. Did Mike meet Ron through you, or did he know Ron before you met Mike?

Oops. Somebody missed one. I also saw this many times while working the crime beat. In their haste, cops will accidentally skip past a name as they decorate their police reports with a black marker. It has happened here. "Name Deleted" now has a first name – "Mike" – but I have no idea why Mr. Baker is asking Kim questions about a man she dated a few times back in 1992. Very strange.

A. Can you say that again.

Q. I'm not sure I even understood it. Did [Name Deleted] know Ron prior to the first time you ever met [Name Deleted]?

A. No.

Q. Did you introduce Mike and Ron?

A. No.

Q. How did they meet?

A. I was told in Los Angeles.

Q. Do you know what Mike did for a living when he came to Los Angeles?

A. Not specifically.

Oops. It happens again. Still, I have no idea who Mike is, and why Mr. Baker is bringing him up. I am about to find out.

Q. What understanding do you have at all about his employment in Los Angeles?

A. That he wanted to do acting.

Q. Do you know if he was successful?

A. No, I don't know.

Q. *What do you know at all about [Name Deleted] after he moved to Los Angeles?*

A. *That he was killed.*

Q. *Anything else?*

A. *He got Ron a job at Mezzaluna.*

Q. *Did you ever hear that he was a club promoter?*

A. *No.*

Q. *Did [Name Deleted] work at Mezzaluna prior to Ron?*

A. *I don't know.*

Q. *How did [Name Deleted] get Ron a job at Mezzaluna, if you know?*

A. *I don't think I know.*

Q. *Do you know anything about [Name Deleted]'s death?*

A. *Yes.*

Q. *What do you know?*

A. *He was shot.*

Q. *Do you know when this occurred?*

A. *Sometime throughout the course of the criminal case.*

Q. *1994, 1995?*

A. *Sometime in '95.*

Q. *Were you ever questioned regarding that case?*

A. *No.*

Hold up. Pause. Pause. Pause. I am sort of in a state of bewilderment at this moment. So let me get this straight. There is some other young man — a guy who also worked at Mezzaluna — a guy who knew Ron and got him the job at Mezzaluna — a guy who went on a blind date with Ron's sister before that — a guy who is shot to death in 1995 while the criminal trial is still underway? Somebody named Mike? You have to be kidding me. What the heck?

Once again, I am drawing a complete blank. I do not remember anything about a former Mezzaluna waiter being murdered. Armed with only the name "Mike," I do a quick Google search: "Mike Mezzaluna Murder."

The first link that pops up in my search is a Wikipedia entry titled, "Killing of Michael Nigg." The first paragraph reads:

> *Michael Nigg (April 28, 1969 – September 8, 1995) was an aspiring actor who worked as a waiter at a Beverly Hills restaurant. He was shot and killed during an apparent robbery attempt in Hollywood. The Los Angeles Police Department later arrested three suspects but soon released them for lack of evidence. No other suspects have ever been identified, and the killing remains unsolved.*

Again, I am at a loss. Michael Nigg? That name does not ring a bell. Not even close . . . and he was murdered on Sept. 8, 1995? That is near the very end of the criminal trial! The case is unsolved? His killers are still out there somewhere? Is this even real?

The Wikipedia entry is not very long. The last heading reads: "Possible Connection to the O.J. Simpson Murder Case." As a high school English teacher, I can tell you that

I did not allow my students to use Wikipedia as a source. I warned them that some of the information they might share from this source on their research papers could be suspect. As a result, I must proceed with caution myself.

At the bottom, the entry references a 2008 book titled "When The Husband Is A Suspect?" which claims that the Mezzaluna restaurant was a "nexus for drug trafficking in Brentwood." I find this portion of the book on the web, and it states, "Reports suggested that several employees of the Mezzaluna were connected to the drug trade or to the Mafia." I realize quickly that I am about to go deep into some conspiracy crap. Now we are trying to involve the Mafia? Of course, it offers no specifics of these so-called "reports." Still, I want to know more about Michael Nigg. Keep reading.

Wikipedia attributes another book, Killing Time, in which an "unnamed source" claims Michael Nigg previously lived in Colorado, and was "known to law enforcement there to be involved in the narcotics culture in Aspen." I do not trust unnamed sources, and I do not trust the stench coming from these words, but my curiosity on Michael Nigg just continues to grow. I am able to get my hands on this book published in 1996. I find Nigg's name mentioned twice — on pages 149 and 233.

> *"Michael Nigg, a fellow waiter at Mezzaluna, was gunned down in Hollywood by killers unknown in September 1995. According to authorities in the Aspen and Denver areas, Nigg was involved in the narcotics culture of Colorado."*

Authorities in the Aspen and Denver areas? What authorities? Is anybody going to actually name a source?

I immediately call bullshit. However, since I paid for the book, I might as well just go ahead and thumb over to Page 233, which lists Michael Nigg as a "lead to pursue." Apparently, nobody takes the authors up on their recommendation, which, to me, says a lot.

> *"Was the Nigg murder, in fact, a random crime? There are telling indications to the contrary: no robbery; a second person left unharmed; a getaway car; the killers who just 'walked' away."*

So dramatic. This page in "Killing Time," written by Donald Freed and Dr. Raymond P. Briggs, also has a reference to an Associated Press story about Michael Nigg's murder. Maybe I can find the story on the web. By this time, I have forgotten about Ron Goldman's travel patterns. I want to know more about the Michael Nigg case. I figure I can trust the information that Associated Press provides as accurate, and it does not take long to find the AP story on the web.

The AP story, dated Sept. 12, 1995, is about 26-year-old Michael Nigg, who is murdered on Sept. 8 after withdrawing $40 from an ATM to take his girlfriend to a Hollywood restaurant. Detectives are looking for three men, including two attackers and a driver.

The story also mentions that Mickey Rourke was among friends holding a candlelight vigil the following evening at the parking lot where Nigg was killed. In a televised plea, Rourke urges anyone with information to come forward. The article also includes a quote from a coworker named Marika Repasi, who describes Nigg as "... a gentleman, very, very positive, upbeat."

Nigg worked as a waiter at Mezzaluna, the article states, and befriended Goldman before quitting in May, 1994.

As I read the quote from Marika Repasi, his co-worker, it begins to sink in that Michael Nigg was a real person with real friends and family who loved him. Just like Ron Goldman, Michael and I would be about the same age if alive today.

As a side note, I end up finding a phone number for Ms. Repasi a few years later. I send her a text asking for an interview. She effectively declines my request, but she does send me a photo of Michael.

I can sit and watch hours and hours of true crime documentaries on almost a daily basis. Like many of us, I have probably been introduced to hundreds of murder cases by now through the media. Why is there nothing out there about Michael Nigg? At first glance, his case does appear to have some intrigue. For starters, there is the Ron Goldman connection. It is also interesting to know from the Wikipedia entry that police arrest three suspects and later release them. I bet there is a good story there. The AP story also names Mickey Rourke as one of Michael's friends. That is pretty cool. Is there really nothing on the ID channel about this case?

Wait a minute. Mickey Rourke? He was friends with Mickey Rourke? Didn't Mickey Rourke have a little bit of a drug problem in the mid-1990s? I find a 2016 article in the New York Post about an upcoming book by Lenny Dykstra, a former All-Star outfielder who hits rock bottom after his retirement. In the book, Dykstra talks about going on a 10-day cocaine binge with Rourke and company at a Beverly Hills hotel. There is that "C" word again.

"Mickey and I went on a 10-day run of partying.
Mickey had his crew of Hollywood wannabes, bottom

feeders who clung to him like s--t on a shoe, and we
were all hitting the [cocaine] nonstop."

Dykstra also tells Howard Stern that Rourke owes him $30,000 for the hotel bill afterward. In a video that goes viral, Rourke threatens to "rip him a new asshole" if he ever sees him again. Still, I wonder how Rourke knows Michael Nigg. Why is this huge celebrity speaking to the press at a candlelight vigil for a Beverly Hills waiter and aspiring actor?

It would sure be nice to talk to Mickey Rourke about Michael Nigg, but how in the world do I get a hold of him? I find a name for his publicist, Dima McKinney, on the web, and then I check to see if the publicist is anywhere on social media. Sure enough . . . there he is. I send McKinney a message asking if he can relay my inquiry about Michael Nigg to the actor. I am surprised how fast I get a response.

"He said he doesn't know this name. It doesn't sound familiar."

Weird. I know it was nearly 30 years ago, but you would think Mickey would remember speaking at a candlelight vigil for one of his murdered friends. Then again, Mickey could have forgotten a few things from those difficult days. Maybe Mickey just happened to be in the neighborhood on the night of the candlelight vigil and then offered his help with the TV news crew.

I just have to know more about this murder case. Maybe I need to start thinking and acting more like a crime reporter. Maybe I need to talk to LAPD, but how do I get through the front door? I am nobody. I am a school principal in Arizona. I have not carried a press credential in years.

I search the web some more and find an article in LA Magazine about a man named Rick Jackson, a retired LAPD detective who has been dubbed "The Godfather" of Los Angeles crime writers. According to this article, Jackson provides expertise to crime writers who want their creative work to be realistic and accurate. It also says Jackson previously worked in Robbery-Homicide Division, so I suppose it is possible he has some direct knowledge of the case.

Just like Mickey Rourke, my next challenge is getting him on the phone somehow.

Near the end of the article, it mentions that Jackson married a woman in the Bay Area and now works part-time investigating cold cases for the San Mateo County Sheriff's Office. Sure enough, I find his name and phone number on the department web site.

However, as I reach for the phone, I have to ask myself an important question now. What in the heck am I doing? Why am I bothering this important person who is attempting to bring some sense of closure to grieving families of unsolved murder victims in his county. Again, I am nobody. What am I going to tell him? "Oh, I'm just curious." At this point, I realize it is time to make a commitment. It is time to chase after one of my lifelong dreams. Before I call Rick Jackson, I send a text to my fiancé:

"Babe, I am going to write a book about all this. I am really going to do it."

I call the number and leave a message for Rick. A few hours later, he calls me back. He is a total professional and genuinely interested in my inquiry. I really appreciate that. I ask if there is any chance he is familiar with a Hollywood cold case involving a victim named Michael Nigg. I do not mention any reported links to the O.J. Simpson case. I am not sure why, but it just does not seem right at the time.

Jackson tells me is not familiar with the Michael Nigg case.

"However, I still know some people over there in homicide," Jackson says. "Let me make some phone calls and I will get back to you."

You have to understand . . . just having this man take me seriously is a victory and a major vote of confidence for me.

Three days later, I am sitting on a chair getting my eyes examined by a doctor. My cell phone rings. The caller ID provides a name: Richard Jackson. I apologize to the doctor and run outside to take the call.

"Hello, Rick."

"Hi Brian. Hey, I think I hit the jackpot for you."

Rick describes to me a phone conversation he has with a detective named Scott Masterson, who works cold cases for LAPD's West Bureau when he has time.

> *Masterson: "Rick, you are not going to believe this, but I have Nigg's case file open on my desk as we speak. Who is asking?"*

> *Rick: I don't really know. He is a school principal in Arizona. He says he is working on a book."*

It is impossible to describe the acceleration I am feeling at this moment. Is this really happening? There is only one thing left to ask Rick.

"Sooooooo . . . is he willing to give me an interview?"

"Yep, here is his phone number."

Thank heavens I have a pen in my front pants pocket. I write the number on my hand, and then I thank Rick profusely for his help. He really is "The Godfather."

CHAPTER 5 – THE INTERVIEW

Thanks to Rick "The Godfather" Jackson, I am now moments away from my big phone interview, and I have a long list of questions prepared. The receptionist at West Bureau Homicide patches me through to Detective Scott Masterson.

This *is* really happening.

I already have a rough idea of what Masterson looks like because I find a photo of him on the web from 2010. The photo shows Masterson waiting to arrest Dr. Conrad Murray in connection with the death of none other than Michael Jackson. A jury will later find Murray guilty of involuntary manslaughter after he administers a powerful anesthetic as a sleeping agent, leading to Jackson's death on June 25, 2009. Murray ends up serving less than half of a four-year sentence.

Masterson is also a key prosecution witness in the "Hollywood Obsession Murder Trial" in 2023. A jury finds defendant Gareth Pursehouse guilty in the brutal murder of Dr. Amie Harwick, a popular Hollywood sex therapist.

I start the phone interview by asking Masterson for a little personal background. I learn that he is married with three children. He worked in LAPD for more than three decades after graduating from the academy in 1988. He started as a patrolman before he was asked to work some detective assignments. In 1994, he was assigned to South Bureau Homicide as a full detective. While the bulk of his homicide cases at this time are gang-related drive-by shootings, Masterson was certainly aware of the *big* murder investigation up north in Brentwood.

On the day of my interview, Masterson works for the West Bureau. He and his partner take on cold cases as time permits.

As Masterson dives into some specifics about the Nigg murder case, I quickly realize that I am not going to get all I need in one phone interview. We are talking about a complicated murder case with all sorts of details – too many to transfer over the phone in one sitting. I know I will likely have to ask for more interviews, preferably in person, if I am going to do this job right.

Masterson tells me he had no knowledge of the Nigg murder case until 2018, when he received a phone call from a woman involved in a purse snatching many years ago.

"From talking to her, she knew about the Nigg case and felt there was a connection," Masterson said. "That's when I pulled the case off the shelf, blew the dust off, and started reading through it."

While I am thrilled to have any new information that is not readily available to the public, Masterson is careful about revealing too much too soon while he re-investigates the case. I do learn that Nigg and his girlfriend, identified as Julie Long, planned to go to dinner that night at the El Coyote Restaurant. Michael finds a small parking lot nearby on Poinsettia Place. As he exits the vehicle, Masterson says, two adult Black males confront him.

"A struggle ensued and one shot was heard," Masterson

says. "That's when Mr. Nigg fell to the ground."

I continue to type as fast as I can as Masterson offers more and more details. After a while, I decide it is finally time to get it out of the way and ask a couple of *juicy* questions from my list. Is the detective aware that Michael Nigg knew Ron Goldman? Does he think the two murders are connected somehow?

"I've heard that through interviews, and that Mr. Nigg also worked at the Mezzaluna Restaurant at one time," Masterson said. "My investigation doesn't show this case is related to that case in any way. It plays no role in his death."

At this moment, I do not think I fully appreciate the weight of this last statement. Almost everything on the web about Michael Nigg attempts to connect his death with the O.J. case, even though there are zero facts to back these "alternative theories."

Now I have an actual LAPD cold case detective, on the record, who is effectively squashing one of the many conspiracy theories put forth by people like Donald Freed and Dr. Raymond P. Briggs, the authors of "Killing Time." The book is touted as the "The First Full Investigation" into the murders of Ron and Nicole, including a haphazard look at Michael Nigg shooting on Sept. 8, 1995.

"Was the Nigg murder, in fact, a random crime? . . . "

Well, Mr. Freed and Dr. Briggs, I hate to break it to you, and I know this is not very sexy, but the answer to your question is . . . yes. It was a random crime. It was also brutal, senseless and cowardly, and whoever committed the despicable act is getting away with it – to this day.

More importantly, it just *feels* like few people care.

Ron Goldman and Michael Nigg had so much in common. They were about the same age. Their murders took place about 15 months and 10 miles apart. Ron and Michael had some of the same dreams and aspirations. They worked the same types of jobs to make ends meet. They were both young and handsome with charming personalities. They knew each other. Michael even dated Ron's sister!

Yet, for whatever reason, Ron Goldman is still a household name 30 years after his death, while Michael Nigg is nowhere on the public radar – except for when a conspiracy theorist mentions his name.

I never met Michael, or his family and friends, but I have to believe he deserves something better. I realize now this project I am working on might just have a purpose – to introduce the world to Michael's story and possibly get somebody to start talking. Maybe somebody out there knows something that will bring his killers to justice.

Then again, maybe justice is coming sooner than I realize.

As I wrap up what I hope will be the first of several interviews, Detective Masterson lets me in on a little secret that almost goes over my head at first.

"You might want to hurry up with your book because I am about to file," Masterson says.

At first, I am not certain what the detective is telling me. These days, when I hear the word *file*, I think about income taxes and computers.

"Wait a minute, do you mean file charges?" I ask.

"That is correct."

Masterson then explains to me that law enforcement did not fully analyze all of the evidence collected at the Michael Nigg crime scene. He has already forwarded that evidence to the Forensic Science Division for DNA testing – an investigative tool that was still relatively new to law enforcement in the mid-1990s. Just ask the folks from the O.J. trial.

I have already learned through my initial web searches that LAPD arrested three suspects in the Michael Nigg case, ". . . but soon released them for lack of evidence." However, what I do not realize at the time of this interview with Masterson is just *how much* LAPD believed it had caught the killers. All I do know at this time is that Masterson believes he is about to put a slam-dunk on another cold case, and now the old newshound from Parker, Arizona is ready to pounce. If Masterson really is about to make some arrests, and even though I no longer work in the news media, I still want "the scoop." I ask the detective for a small favor. Since I am the only one asking him about Michael Nigg, would he be willing to give me the exclusive when it all goes down? I figure I still have a few contacts in the media world, and it would give my book a little more credibility if I can show I broke this story.

"Sure." he says.

As we wrap up the interview, I start to envision myself walking into somewhere like the LA Times as a "freelance reporter," offering to give them my news story in exchange for a byline and maybe a few extra bucks. The LA Times has actually paid me for a story before – 50 bucks for covering a high school basketball game in Fresno in the mid-1990s.

Any good desk editor is certain to want *this* story about LAPD making arrests for Michael Nigg's murder almost three decades after the fact. An even better desk editor is certain to ask for photos. I decide to push my luck a little with Masterson and request one last favor.

"When you do make an arrest," I ask, "how would you feel about me being there with a camera?"

"That shouldn't be a problem," Masterson says. "Just be ready, because when I get the OK from the district attorney, you will have about 24 hours to get out here."

Twenty-four hours? I do not need that much time.

"I can be there in five."

As soon as I hang up the phone, I immediately start making plans for a quick trip to Los Angeles at a moment's notice. Although he offers no timeline, Masterson gives me the impression an arrest could be just a few days away. My boss, although I am sure he thinks I have gone off the deep end, gives me permission ahead of time to leave campus when the time comes. I pack an overnight bag and put it in the trunk of my car. My school librarian offers to let me borrow her digital camera.

I even type up a press release that is ready to go in a moment's notice after I fill in a few blanks, such as the suspects' names. It has all the background and some quotes from Masterson. The headline of the press release reads:

"Arrests Made In '95 Hollywood Cold Case"

I am all ready. All I can do now is wait.

As an Air Force veteran, I am used to a little "hurry up and wait," so it does not really bother me when a few days turn into a week, or when a few weeks turn into a month. Besides, I still have other things I can do, like go back to my original question and find out how Ron Goldman got to Nicole's condo. It is during this waiting period, in fact, that I inadvertently begin another unexpected adventure, even more bizarre and extremely explosive. More on that later.

On Nov. 3, 2021, I decide to send Detective Masterson just a quick email asking if there happens to be any updates to the Michael Nigg cold case. I do not want to come across as impatient, even though that is exactly what is happening. A week later, I get a response:

Good morning Mr. Wedemeyer

Sorry I have not returned your email until today. I have been waiting to hear back from the Forensic Science Division. I requested additional testing on some evidence that was originally collected at the crime scene. I just got the reports this morning from FSD that some previously untested evidence has developed DNA. This new DNA has now been submitted to CODIS for possible identification. After the CODIS run is completed I will be in a better position to talk with you.

Take care

Scott Masterson

I am somewhat familiar with CODIS (Combined DNA Index System) from watching true crime TV. The FBI introduced this national DNA database in 1998, and by the time of Detective Masterson's email, it has surpassed 20 million DNA profiles collected. If Michael Nigg's killers left some DNA at the crime scene, there is a chance it will match a profile or two in CODIS. Masterson obviously expects a match.

The wait continues . . . December . . . January . . . no additional word from Detective Masterson.

On Feb. 25, 2022, I finally decide to send the detective another quick email.

Good morning Scott,

I'm just checking in with you to see if there are any updates regarding the Michael Nigg case.

Have a great day.

A few weeks later, I get a response:

"Hi Brian

Sorry for the delay in getting back to you, I just got back from an investigative trip to New Mexico.

As to the Nigg investigation. It is getting compli- cated because I am still working some complicated leads that have taken a lot longer to flush out than I thought. What is complicating things is that I am retiring very soon and moving out of state. I had hoped to have had all this settled long ago. My con- cern is I don't have the time to do what the case needs and I will retire and the case will be put back on the shelf. As you know LAPD considers the case closed, "Cleared Other". Having said all that I have a meeting with my LAPD boss to discuss the case and what I need.

Sorry I can not give you a better answer at this time.

At this point, two things come to mind. First, it definitely ap- pears there are not going to be any arrests any time soon. Second, Masterson is getting ready to ride off into the sunset. If I have any other questions, I better catch him first.

I respond with a list of questions for my book, assum- ing an arrest is not going to happen. I ask him if he is will- ing to part with any photos from the crime scene. I ask him for his personal opinion on the case. I ask him for a better description of the suspects. I ask him for any leads he thinks I should chase after he is gone.

On April 15, 2022, I receive my last communication from Detective Scott Masterson. It is 3:22 p.m., and school has just ended for the day.

"Hi Brian

Hope you are doing well. I have attached a copy of my report of the Nigg homicide, I hope it helps. If you have any questions please feel free to reach out. My last day at work will be May 31.

Good luck.

Scott Masterson"

As I am sure you can imagine, my chest is pounding as I close my office door and sit back down. I slowly move my cursor up to the attachment that reads "NIGG Report." Here we go . . . and. . . click.

The document, titled "Unsolved Murder Investigation Progress Report," is a whopping 53 pages long. It has every-thing . . . full write-ups on both the initial and follow-up investigations, witness and suspect names, mug shots, police sketches, evidence lists, and crime scene photos, includ-ing some of the deceased. That poor young man. Nobody deserves that.

Now I am fired up. There is no turning back now. I have to get the word out. I have to let people know about Michael.

CHAPTER 6 – KEEP GOING

It is Aug. 16, 2022. Since we are short on bus drivers in our district, my school starts an hour later than our sister schools in town. This gives me an opportunity to treat myself to breakfast from time to time at the Early Bird Diner in Parker, Ariz., and today just happens to be my birthday.

As usual, I take a seat at the counter, which is shaped like a big "U" in the middle of the restaurant. Directly across from me on the other side of the counter are the same two old-timers I always see, loudly sharing their opinions on the many reasons they think our great nation is dying a quick death. As they converse, they are watching the news on a small TV above my head.

I order a simple two-egg breakfast with hash browns, biscuits and gravy, a side of bacon, and a large Diet Pepsi that I will refill at least three times. As usual, my big plate of food arrives quickly. This is one of those old-school diners where the employees take their job seriously. All the servers are experienced and friendly. They know most of the patrons at the counter on a first name basis, although I have not quite reached that status, yet.

For fun, I break up my bacon slices into smaller pieces and carefully shape them into a "53" over the top of my breakfast. I am an obsessed fan of "Breaking Bad," arguably the greatest TV show of all time, and its lead character, Walter White, who started his birthdays in the same manner. I take a photo of my "Breakfast Bad" masterpiece and post it on Facebook for the world to see. I know. Dumb. The bacon does not last long after that.

As I enjoy my birthday breakfast and read about another Arizona Diamondbacks loss from the night before on my cell phone, my conservative "counter" parts are not-so-quietly solving our country's immigration issues. It does not take long before a cowbell attached to the front door of the diner sounds off, and a sharply dressed stranger walks in. He seems to have captured everybody's attention at the diner, except for maybe the two good 'ole boys across from me.

The man is about my age, wearing what appears to be a very expensive, light-blue business suit with matching tie. There is not a store within 100 miles that sells suits like that. Instead of leather shoes, he is wearing white sneakers, and for some reason, it looks pretty darn cool. In fact, I am a little envious. I would love to wear a suit like that – just for a day. Instead, I am showcasing the same damn Dockers I always do, with some Walmart shoes and a black polo shirt with my school's logo on the front. The man is obviously in great shape, and his custom-made suit fits him like a glove. Well, maybe not O.J.'s glove. He looks like he could be a former pro wide receiver ready to pal around with Howie Long, Michael Strahan and company on the set of NFL Fox Sunday.

The mystery man sits down next to me to my right at the only empty counter seat available, and I immediately notice his watch. It must be worth thousands of dollars. He has dark hair with a touch of gray combed to one side. The waitress smiles as she lays a menu on the counter in front of him. He says good morning to her, then he turns to me and offers the same greeting. I am glad I finished off my bacon before he sat down and noticed my plate.

It turns out our mystery man is only here for a quick cup of coffee. I hear him chuckle to himself a bit as the old-timers strategize over a proper border wall design. He gulps down his coffee and gives the waitress a $100 bill.

"I would also like to buy this guy's breakfast, and please, keep the change," he tells her.

Before I even realize what is happening, he stands up and pats me on the shoulder as he walks behind me towards the door. I tell him thank you, but I am not sure if he hears me. For some reason, my eyes continue to follow him. As he opens the door and the cowbell rings, the man turns back towards me and nods his head with a confident grin of approval.

"Keep going," he says.

Just like that, the man is gone. Keep going? What does that mean? Suddenly, it hits me. Could it really be him? Is that even possible? I jump out of my seat and make my way to the exit, where an elderly man is now holding the door open for his wife, who is using a walker. I cannot get through the doorway at this very moment, but I can see the man walking towards a gold Mercedes Benz in the small parking lot.

By the time I make it outside, he is opening his driver's side door.

"Excuse me . . . sir?"

Again, the man does not hear me. He ducks down into his seat, and before the driver's side door closes, I give it one more try.

"Michael?!"

Just like that, the man is gone. The vehicle exits the parking lot and turns west on the main drag going through town. Yes, west . . . towards Southern California.

I should note that the vast majority of my dreams usually disappear from my memory in an instant. Yet, for some reason, I can recall every detail of this one. Although I do not consider myself of the spiritual sort, my heart tells me that Michael Nigg just walked into, and out of, my dream. In fact, I am certain of it.

Keep going.

To this day, those two words continue to stick with me. I want the world to know Michael Nigg – the man in my dream. I want to replace an irresponsible conspiracy theory about Michael with actual facts. I want to talk to people who loved him and still miss him.

Who was Michael Nigg, the person? What were his likes and dislikes? Michael and I were born 255 days apart. I cannot help but wonder if we would have made friends if we ever crossed paths. Was he a sports fan like me? Did he like the same music? Did he like to go clubbing in Hollywood? That is what I did when I lived in nearby Thousand Oaks, a place where Ronald Goldman taught kids how to play tennis at the time. What was Michael's beer preference? How did he like his steak? I want to know everything. I want you to know everything.

In this current age when true crime fans cannot wait for the next episode of Dateline ID, or the next documentary series on Netflix, or the next podcast of Wine and Crime, why has Michael's unsolved murder been largely ignored. A young, handsome actor with a loose connection to the O.J. case? Isn't that just the kind of cold case that people are looking for? I just do not get it.

Maybe, just maybe, if I can dig up the story of Michael Nigg somehow, and share it with others, maybe somebody will talk. The murderers are very likely still out there. Maybe all this time and energy will lead to justice for Michael someday.

I discover a photo of Michael's gravestone on the web. He is buried at Evergreen Memorial Park in Jefferson County, Colo. It reads:

MICHAEL SCOTT NIGG

APRIL 28, 1969-SEPT. 8, 1995

SON, BROTHER, FRIEND TO ALL

HE LIVED "LIKE HEATED ATOMS,"

CHANGING US WITH HIS LOVE

It just bothers me that nobody stands up for Michael . . . at least not in the public eye. I am starving to speak to a live person who remembers him. There has to be somebody I can find on the Internet. I discover a web site called "Families Of Homicide Victims And Missing Persons," which advocates for families of 1,750 cold case murder victims from Colorado since 1970. The web site includes a short profile on Michael, including a little more information than what is found in the Wikipedia blurb.

". . . Nature was an important part of his life. He

liked skiing and played soccer from age 6 to 18. His favorite retreat was in the mountains. Michael was always available to be a friend; he always had time for others . . . "

The profile ends by identifying Michael's parents – Gayle Hart of Littleton, Colo., and Joseph Nigg of Denver. I have to find them. I have to keep going. By now, I have purchased a web site that performs minimal background checks on people. I am able to find phone numbers, current and former addresses, even some criminal records if they exist.

I start with Gayle Hart, and immediately find a recent number for her. I leave a message.

"Hello, Gayle. My name is Brian Wedemeyer. I am working on a book project and I would like to know if you would be open to an interview about your son. Could you please give me a call at (phone number)? Thank you. I look forward to hearing from you."

The return phone call never comes, so after a few days, I leave another message. Then another. Nothing.

Finally, on a Sunday morning, I decide to give it one more try. A woman with a soft voice is on the other end.

"Hello?"

Oh my. This is the moment. This is my chance to learn about Michael from his own mother. As politely and respectfully as I possibly can, I give her my little introduction and ask her for an interview. Gayle responds with silence.

"Gayle? Did I lose you?"

Click.

As disappointing as this is, I do feel a weird sense of

accomplishment. I finally spoke to someone who knew Michael. . . even if she did not speak back. It drives home the point that Michael is more than a Wikipedia blurb. He is a man who was loved and cared for. There are people on this planet who are still hurting from his murder.

The hunt for Michael's father does not take long. I search the web and immediately find a Joseph Nigg, who happens to be an accomplished author and an expert on mythical monsters of all things. He has written numerous books, translated into multiple languages, on how creatures like dragons, unicorns, gryphons and other "fantastic animals" first appear in various cultures.

Joseph Nigg wrote his first book, titled *The Book of Gryphons*, about eagle-lion creatures, in 1982. His most recent book is a non-fiction piece published in 2016, titled *The Phoenix: An Unnatural Biography of a Mythical Piece*. On his web site, www.josephnigg.com, the book receives strong praise from a man named Joseph Hutchison.

"*The Phoenix* is honestly the best book of its kind that I've read since Joseph Campbell's The Hero of a Thousand Faces," Hutchison writes.

I also find a 2019 podcast called "The Monster Professor" on youtube.com in which Mr. Nigg is the special guest.

"That's what I like most about these creatures," Nigg tells the interviewer. ". . . it's following them through time and watching their cultural transformations."

Listening to Joseph Nigg's voice, I realize I will be interacting with a very brilliant mind if I can ever get him on the phone. The man has a Ph.D from the University of Denver's writing program, which, quite honestly, is a little intimidating. Still, I cannot wait to find out his thoughts on Michael's case. I also understand the odds are good that he will have no interest in talking to me whatsoever.

I send Joseph Nigg a message on the "contact" page of his web site. Nothing. I try to leave him a phone message. Nothing. I leave a message for him on social media. Nothing. He is not talking to me . . . at least not about Michael.

Shut down again.

I continue searching deep into the web looking for anything with Michael Nigg's name on it. Almost every link deals with the O.J. case and unfounded conspiracy theories.

I discover that Michael Nigg does have a small role in a movie – as a character. That is right. Michael Nigg is a character in the 2019 film, "The Murder of Nicole Brown Simpson," starring actress Mena Suvari, who is probably best known for her work in "American Beauty" as well as "American Pie." IMBD writes:

> *"Inspired by true events, the film follow's OJ Simpson's ex-wife Nicole Brown Simpson in the last days before her tragic death on June 12ᵗʰ, 1994, as seen from her point of view."*

True events? Eh. For starters, it shows Nicole hooking up with Glen Rogers, the convicted serial killer who reportedly confessed to the murders of Ron and Nicole, and near the end of the movie, it shows a jealous O.J. Simpson storming into the Mezzaluna looking for Ron just prior to the murders. Of course, if that really happened, somebody would have testified to it.

Michael Nigg, played by actor Sky Liam, is Ron Goldman's friend and co-worker at the Mezzaluna, even though Michael, in fact, no longer works there at the time of the murders. When Simpson's character enters the restaurant, Nigg quickly advises him to duck out the back door.

"Oh, dude, fuck, look who is here."

"Who?"

"Your girlfriend's husband. He looks seriously PO'd. You might want to make yourself scarce, man."

Except for a brief appearance at the start of the movie, that is basically the extent of Sky Liam's role. Although I don't expect to get much, I decide it would be interesting to track down the actor. Even though it's a very small role, maybe Sky does a little of his own research on Michael. It doesn't hurt to try. Sure enough, I find Sky on social media and he agrees to a phone interview.

Almost immediately, I am impressed by what a polite young gentleman Sky is. He tells me a little bit about his young career as an actor and writer, including some international films as a skilled martial artist. That's cool! He tells me about his biggest acting role in America to date as the obnoxious antagonist Steve Pelski in the 2018 film, "The Amityville Murders," directed by Daniel Farrands.

"I was able to be totally unleashed and go a little crazy in that role," Sky says. "When you get a role where you can just be very irreverent, it's quite fun actually."

Farrands invites Sky to audition for the role of Ron Goldman in his next film, "The Murder of Nicole Brown Simpson."

"He called me a month later and told me the part had already been cast, but there was this other part, which was Michael Nigg, which he wanted me to play. He told me

Michael was a real person, so I looked him up and there wasn't a ton of info. Some of it was obviously kind of hearsay."

You got that right, Sky.

Sky describes the movie itself as a more of a supernatural what-if story, rather than an actual bio film. He understands that many of the details offered are based very loosely on facts.

"All I can remember now is that Michael was killed at an ATM, and I don't think the cash was ever taken," Sky says.

Sky is unaware the murders took place in a parking lot across the street from El Coyote, a restaurant he says he frequents often.

As we are talking, it occurs to me how similar Sky is to Michael at the time of his death. Although he has never waited tables, Sky has worked various jobs to make ends meet while pursuing his filmmaking dreams. In addition to working as a fitness trainer, Sky also receives money to host some live events in the Chinese community of Monterey Park. He studied Mandarin in college.

As for his role in "The Murder of Nicole Brown Simpson," Sky says he earned about 1,000 bucks.

"I'm sure I paid the rent with it."

I have one last question for Sky, who along with O.J. Simpson, happens to be a USC graduate.

"Oh. . . I think OJ did it," he says. "Believe me. Nobody on that set was talking about conspiracy theories."

As I am just about end my search for Michael, I stumble across a poem written by another Joseph. It is Joseph Hutchison – the same man who praises Joseph Nigg's latest book on his web site. A poem in memory of Michael Nigg. A poem about a dream. A poem called "The Blue."

I am not the type of person to get emotional over a poem, and I am certainly not adept at interpreting them. As a high school English teacher, I tended to lean on my journalism roots. Poetry and Shakespeare are not my thing.

However, after reading this poem, I realize I do have a little something in common with Mr. Hutchinson, who happens to be the former Poet Laureate of Colorado with at least 17 published collections. This young man, Michael Nigg, came to us both – and eventually slipped away from us both – in a vivid and memorable dream.

Unlike Joseph Nigg, I am able to track down Hutchison and secure a phone interview. My goal? Find out everything I possibly can about Michael, the person.

As I expected, Hutchison is also quite the gentleman. He shares stories with me about how he met Michael's father in the late 1970s, and how they became colleagues and later the best of friends. He tells me how he met Michael for the first time when Joseph Nigg started hosting get-togethers at his house for local writers.

"Michael was very charming, and he was very smart," Hutchison says. "He was a little hyper, and sometimes he had trouble focusing."

Hutchison also shares stories about how helpful Michael was during Thanksgiving dinners. He describes how Michael would always pitch in on preparing the food and serving the guests. He tells me how Michael worked at a high-end restaurant/pub known as Reiver's before eventually getting the "acting bug" and moving to Southern California.

The interview is off to a great start, but it takes an awkward turn when Hutchison decides to ask me a question.

"Have you talked to his parents?"

I explain to Hutchison how hard I tried getting an

interview with both Joseph and Gayle, but I can tell he feels like he has overstepped his bounds. I do not want to be the cause of a damaged friendship, so I agree to put the interview on hold. I ask Hutchison if he can help me get Joseph Nigg on the phone. He says he will try, and I never hear from either of them.

Based on what I have learned so far, it does not sound like Michael would have trouble making friends – but where are they? It is not until I get the full investigative report from Detective Masterson that I start to learn about some other people in his life at the time. One of those people is a friend named Jay Spence. I do not find Jay, but I am able to connect with his little sister, Cassandra, on social media.

"I was only 9 when this happened and don't remember a ton," Cassandra writes. "My brother Jay though was very upset and hurt for a long time. He loved Mikey and had always had a deep love for any of his friends."

Cassandra also informs me that Jay himself died in a car accident in 2003.

"I was 16 at the time and have never really recovered from it. We all miss him immensely."

Cassandra also connects me with Mindy Myers Lage, who actually moved to California with Michael and Jay in 1991. Mindy was one of Jay's best friends. She tells me Jay met Michael during his freshman year at Western Colorado University, home of the Mountaineers. The three of them lived in Santa Barbara for a few years before Michael and Jay moved into Los Angeles. Mindy would eventually move east to Des Moines, Iowa.

"I don't even know how you would represent Michael in written word because he was so dynamic, positive, charismatic, explosive. And I'm not just waxing nostalgic," Mindy writes. "I don't know how easy it will be to get people to talk about him, but if you can, I believe you'll have a picture of Michael that you never anticipated when you started this journey.

"Jay was equally dynamic. They were quite the duo."

As for the unsupported allegations that Michael was some sort of a cocaine dealer involved in the "narcotics culture of Colorado," as reported in the book, Killing Time by Donald Freed and Raymond P. Briggs, Mindy sets the record straight.

"He never lived in Aspen that I know of . . . He also never did any drugs or drug dealing the whole time we lived together/knew each other besides maybe occasionally smoking some weed, but we were college kids. He was super into health, fitness and working out together, and his body was truly his temple."

Mindy offers to help me connect with other people who were in Michael's life, but I never hear another word. By this point, I feel like I have one person left to find . . .

Julie.

Based on all the conspiracy theories that have tarnished Michael's name and added more pain to those who loved him, I can almost predict that Julie will never talk to me, and that is only if I can find her, but I have to try.

I will later discover, through a completely bizarre coincidence, that Julie Long is now Julie Mills. That is helpful. I track down a phone number for her and leave a message. A web search leads me to what might be her workplace, so I attempt to send her an email. After a few days with no response, I call her office and leave a message.

On a Saturday morning, I receive an email from Julie, and she is not very happy with me. Rather than paraphrase,

I think it is best to share her entire email.

"Hello Brian,

I received a message recently that you are reaching out to me via my place of business. Please do not contact me ever again. Especially at my place of employment.

So many LIES & CONSPIRACY THEORIES surrounding my heartbreak loss that I hope this sets the record STRAIGHT.

1. This was a RANDOM mugging/robbery

2. Michael was driving MY Mercedes. This Mercedes was NOT his car.

3. There is ZERO connection to Michael's random mugging and Ron Goldman & Nicole Brown Simpson murders.

4. Michael was NOT best friends with Ron Goldman. Michael worked a SHORT time at Mezza Luna

5. Michael was NEVER a drug runner that these horrible conspiracy theories have been spread about him. This is absolute BS. I just read a Wikipedia about him and it just contained LIES!

6. Michael was my future and this senseless/random act took that future away from the both of us. He was the kindest, loving, devoted, committed and amazing human being. I miss him every day and just want to live in PEACE.

7. Please do not dishonor my love's honor and reputation any longer by keeping these CONSPIRACY THEORIES alive.

8. Again, this is an unsolved case because it was a RANDOM mugging/robbery."

This email hits me hard, and makes me really question what I am doing. I have never witnessed the pain of irresponsible conspiracy theories on grieving loved ones. Now I see it up close and personal, and it is even directed at me. I feel like I am in a very difficult position. I understand why so many of his loved ones just want to be left alone, even after all these years, but I also *truly* believe that justice is still possible for Michael.

Keep going.

I feel compelled to respond by email to Julie to clear the air. After this, unless she *wants* to talk, I will not bother her. The most important thing I try to convey is that I agree with every one of her points. I explain that I will be very clear to say in this book that there is no connection between Michael's murder and the OJ case. I tell her how my fiancé and I recently visited the crime scene in Hollywood, and I am hoping she can help put some of those details into perspective.

". . . Finally, I am really sorry for your loss. If you do not respond, you will never hear from me again."

A few days later, I receive another email from Julie. Her tone is much different this time around.

"Hello Brian,

I appreciate you responding. I apologize that you received the wrath of 27 years of Michael being dishonored by these conspiracy theories.

I am not sure if writing a book would help solve this case. From my understanding, this is a case that lacks evidence to stand up in court. I would love to be able to delete all of the lies that have been spread.

I have to sit with this for a few days. I will definitely get back to you.

Thank you for your kind words and also for giving me insight to your intentions.

Thank you,

Julie

Julie Mills never does get back to me, and that is OK. I could never imagine the pain she endured on the night of Sept. 8, 1995, not to mention all the "absolute BS" that follows. I just hope she understands . . .

I have to keep going . . . for Michael.

CHAPTER 7 — STACY

I will soon come to learn about another person on the other side of the country who has a very keen interest in Michael Nigg. Without this woman, Michael's case never reaches the desk of Detective Scott Masterson.

To understand and appreciate who this woman is, I have to go back to Sept. 8, 1995 in Hollywood, Calif. It is a few minutes before 10 p.m. Stacy Bartell, a 25-year-old waitress who has dreams of becoming an actress, exits the Caffé Luna Restaurant on Melrose Avenue with her two friends – Emma Maki, 27, and Lee Palmer, 31. They have just treated themselves to one of this trendy restaurant's fabulous desserts.

Like most Friday evenings, it is difficult to find parking on Melrose — one of Southern California's most popular streets. As a result, Stacy's vehicle is more than a block away on Gardner Street in a dimly lit residential area.

The women proceed west on Melrose a few hundred feet before making an immediate turn north on Gardner Street. The upscale neighborhood gets eerily quiet in a hurry as the women create some distance from the many sights and sounds of Melrose.

Soon after they cross Waring Avenue, Emma notices two Black men approaching quickly from the rear. By the time Stacy turns around, one of the men is standing directly in front of her.

"I whirled around and he was already there," says Stacy, who is now a stay-at-home-mom living in Fairfax, Va. "He was a very big guy, and he was very close to me. He was in my personal space."

Stacy leans back slightly as the suspect throws a punch that just misses her face, striking her in the shoulder instead. She is surprised she is still standing. The suspect quickly grabs Stacy's purse strap and pulls so hard that it rips some of the skin off her right arm, leaving a heavy burn mark. He now has her purse and all of its contents in his possession.

The two men immediately sprint southbound on Gardner Street, back towards Melrose. At that moment, the women notice a car's headlights switch on.

"They literally dove into the back seat," Stacy says. "They had a getaway car."

However, instead of getting away, the unseen driver proceeds north on Gardner Street, back in the direction of the terrified young women. After a making a quick pass, the driver makes a U-turn, this time slowing down as he approaches the women, who are now ducking down behind a parked car.

"We thought maybe they were going to try and kill us," Stacy recalls. "There were a lot of drive-by shootings going on at that time."

Instead, one of the suspects shouts, "You dumbass White bitches!" before the vehicle turns east on Waring in the direction of La Brea Avenue.

Almost immediately, several people run outside to check

on the commotion. Stacy and her friends are taken into a nearby house, where 911 is called.

The next morning, Stacy is still shaken by the incident when she gets a call at home from a man who identifies himself as Detective Parry from Hollywood Area Homicide.

Parry: *"We have your purse."*

At first, Stacy is impressed by the quick recovery.

"In all of Los Angeles, I couldn't believe they found my purse that fast," she says. "But right away I could tell there was something very serious in his tone."

Stacy: *"Wait, did you just say you were a homicide detective?"*

Parry: *"I don't want to alarm you over the phone. We need you to come down here immediately. We have to ask you some questions right away."*

When Stacy arrives at the police station and sits down with Detective Parry, she instantly notices her purse on his desk. Although her wallet, driver's license, credit cards and money are missing from the purse, police do find Stacy's SAG (Screen Actors Guild) Card and use that to track her down.

Detective Parry then shares some terrible news. Stacy's purse was actually found at the scene of a murder that took place just 40 minutes after she is robbed – about 1 mile south near Poinsettia Place and Beverly Boulevard.

"He told me the victim's name, and how he was on a date with his girlfriend. It was just horrible. I remember thinking that easily could have been me."

The detective interviews Stacy about the purse snatching and gets a physical description of the suspects. Instead of booking the purse into evidence as a potential source of DNA, police give it back to Stacy, who then returns home and waits for news of an arrest. She figures it is only a matter of time before one of the suspects is caught using one of her credit cards.

"But I never heard from anybody . . . ever again."

The purse snatching is not Stacy's first encounter with violent crime. In 1993, she was a hostage during an armed robbery attempt at her workplace.

"The mugging was very bad, but that was much worse," she says. "I feel very lucky to be alive."

The two events have resulted in a "profound" case of PTSD, which is still a big part of her life to this day.

"I don't do great in crowded situations," she says. "I have this feeling that I'm always on the lookout for something bad to happen. When there is a loud, unexpected noise, you can peel me off the ceiling."

Stacy does recall some local media coverage in the immediate wake of Michael Nigg's murder, but nothing more. It is not until 2007 during a random Google search that she learns of reported links between Michael and Ronald Goldman.

"That really bothered me a lot, because I don't want to have even the most peripheral connection to that mess," she says.

However, Stacy is still unaware of one very important detail – a detail she now believes could have helped police solve the case of Michael Nigg's murder.

Nearly a decade later, in 2018, Stacy is watching a news story about O.J. Simpson's release from a Nevada state prison. The story prompts Stacy to return to the internet for any possible updates on Michael's unsolved case. This time around, that important detail, which does not offer much in the way of specifics, is available.

*"The Los Angeles Police Department later arrest-
ed three suspects but soon released them for lack of
evidence."*

Stacy is in shock. She knows she was literally face-to-face
with the man who swiped her purse – the same purse found
at the scene of Michael Nigg's murder just 40 minutes later.
Yet, when police arrest three suspects on Feb. 8, 1996 – just
five months after the murder – nobody from LAPD bothers
to contact her.

"I thought I was going to faint because I never knew that
. . . and nobody called me," she says. "They could have trot-
ted him out in a lineup for me, and I could have said that's
the one! Whoever handled that case . . . the detective who
called to say here's your purse . . . I feel like he dropped the
ball."

On March 16, 2018, Stacy places a call to LAPD and is
connected with none other than Scott Masterson, a cold case
detective with West Bureau Homicide. Stacy shares her story
about the purse snatching on Gardner Street more than 22
years earlier and a young man named Michael Nigg, the ". . .
stranger she has never forgotten." Masterson, a seasoned veteran who has solved other high profile cold cases for LAPD
over the years, digs into the archives and retrieves the file on
Michael's murder. He then books a flight for Virginia.

Detective Masterson re-interviews Stacy before giving her
a look at some photo arrays. He wants to see if Stacy is able
to identify any of the three arrest suspects. The two friends
who went with her to Caffe Luna that night eventually will
also get a look. However, more than two decades of separa-
tion do not offer any help.

"It was very difficult looking at the pictures because it was so far back in time," Stacy says. "There were a couple of photos I felt a ping on, and some of the faces . . . I felt nothing."

Stacy Bartell now goes by her married name of Stacy *Langton*. If that name sounds familiar, it is because she made international news in the fall of 2021 over an incident that occurred at a Fairfax County school board meeting in Virginia. During a call to the public, Stacy appeared at the podium with two books checked out from her son's high school library.

Stacy informed the board that both books contained pornographic material involving sex between men and boys. To prove her point, she shared illustrations from the books and started reading some of the explicit excerpts. Despite Stacy's objections, the Board chairperson cut her time short, pointing out that there were children in the audience.

"It was almost like she was making my point for me," Stacy would later tell an interviewer from Sweden.

Stacy's message was loud and clear, however, as a video clip from the meeting immediately went viral. She would soon give interviews to numerous media outlets, including Fox News.

As a result, when I search the internet for a woman named Stacy Langton, she is everywhere. I can't help but wonder if this is the same Stacy I am looking for. After some digging, I discover a phone number that might be hers. I get a little nervous when I hear a woman's voice on the other end.

I introduce myself as a school principal working on a book in my spare time, and Stacy understandably assumes it has something to do with the school library controversy.

"Actually, you might think this is kind of weird, but I am calling about a homicide that took place in Hollywood in 1995. Any chance you might know what I'm talking about?"

I can hear Stacy take a deep breath over the phone before she responds.

"Oh yes . . . Michael Nigg. I have been waiting for this day."

CHAPTER 8 — LADIES NIGHT

Stacy is not the only woman who gets a good look at one or more potential suspects. Again, we need to go back to Sept. 8, 1995. It is early evening in El Segundo, Calif on Santa Monica Bay. Another intense work week has come to an end at Merisel Inc., one of the world's largest distributors of personal computer hardware and software.

Five co-workers, including Carina Longworth, Dana Bilvado, April Reynolds, Lesley Mobbs and Lisa Schipper, are trying to figure out where to go for happy hour to let off some steam. Lesley and Lisa, who are sisters, mention one of their favorite restaurants – the El Coyote Café in Hollywood.

"They had cheap margaritas and really good food," says Lesley, who is now a vice president at a global investment management company based in Southern California. "But I don't think they're that cheap anymore."

The other women are sold on the idea. The group agrees to take a chance on El Coyote even though it is roughly 45 minutes away – probably longer with all the rush-hour traffic. All five women climb into Carina's white Isuzu Trooper. They are all in their late 20's and early 30's, and alternative rock is the choice of tunes on the radio. U2 happens to be Lesley's favorite.

At about 7 p.m., the women arrive at El Coyote Café at 7312 Beverly Blvd. Lesley and Lisa are accustomed to finding a parking space at the restaurant, or even curbside along Beverly out front. However, on this busy Friday night, available parking is nowhere in sight.

Carina continues east on Beverly before making a quick left turn northbound on Poinsettia Place. Maybe they can find a parking spot on this nearby residential street without having to walk too far back to the restaurant. As soon as they round the corner, they notice a very small parking lot near an alley behind The Art Store to their left. It is after normal business hours, so it should not be a problem parking here. The neighborhood appears fairly affluent, so any thoughts of potential danger or criminal activity never enters their minds.

"It's the shopping capital of the world basically, so it's just not an area where I would feel unsafe," Lesley says.

The women exit the vehicle and walk back towards Beverly Boulevard. They cross the busy street and enter through the front door of the restaurant to find a waiting area that is decorated with photos upon photos of Hollywood stars on the walls and even the ceiling. Let a much-needed evening of fun and laughter begin.

As soon as the women sit down, they order a margarita and start scanning the large menu. Lesley and Lisa already know what they want – one of El Coyote's specialty salads with a side of beans and tortillas. This is just what the women needed to take away some of that work stress. The food, drink and unique atmosphere at this famous restaurant are well worth the long drive. The women definitely plan on coming back in the near future.

After a few hours and a few more margaritas, the women close the tab and exit the restaurant. The laughter continues as the women cross Beverly at Poinsettia Place and make their way to the parking lot.

"I remember we were being really loud and obnoxious," Lisa says.

Just as the women are about to turn the corner behind The Art Store, Lesley is the only woman in the group who notices a vehicle approaching from the opposite direction on Poinsettia Place. The car stops along the curb on Poinsettia next to the parking lot. Two adult Black males immediately exit the vehicle and start walking directly towards the women, who are still laughing and carrying on except for Lesley.

"But at the same time, I'm seeing these guys from the corner of my eye," Lesley says. "I could see that they were making a B-line for us . . . a 100-percent B-line. There is no doubt in my mind they were coming for us. They had intentions of something with us."

Lesley immediately takes charge and gets the attention of her dinner companions. The two men are closing in from just a few hundred feet away. Lesley remembers one of the men wearing a shirt with blue and white stripes.

"Guys, guys, guys! Focus!" Lesley yells. "Get in the car. Pronto. Right now!"

As the women hurry into Carina's Isuzu Trooper and lock the doors, Lesley notices another vehicle – a brand new gold Mercedes Benz sedan – enter the parking lot.

"When these two dudes saw that other vehicle pull in, they immediately changed directions and made a B-line straight for them," Lesley said. "They really quickly redirected. It was like watching a lion going after its prey. They fully had intentions of something. They knew what they were doing. They wanted something."

Still unsure of what is happening, Carina starts to back her vehicle out of the parking stall. In front of her, she briefly notices a Black male standing in the distance. Dana, who is sitting in the front passenger seat, observes another Black male, wearing a T-shirt with horizontal stripes, step in between two parked cars. As Carina's car backs out, she watches the Black male confront a young White male who has just stepped out of the gold Mercedes on the driver's side.

The women hear a loud pop.

Dana watches as the young White male collapses to the pavement. She also sees the young man in the striped shirt quickly walk away from the scene towards Poinsettia Place, followed by a second Black male suspect. At the same time, a woman steps out of the Mercedes on the passenger side, walks around to the driver's side, and begins screaming hysterically.

Lesley does not have as good a view as Dana from her spot on the left rear passenger seat. Inside Carina's Trooper, there is chaos and confusion.

"That was a gunshot!" Lesley screams.

"No it wasn't," another passenger responds.

"Yeah, it was! We gotta call 911."

According to the investigative report, Carina quickly exits the parking lot and turns south on Poinsettia Place before crossing the intersection. She immediately turns into a lighted parking lot at nearby Kearn's Market as Lesley talks to the 911 dispatcher. By this time, several other witnesses have called 911 to report a gunshot as well as suspects fleeing the scene in a vehicle traveling northbound on Poinsettia Place.

The dispatcher directs the women to a nearby police station to provide witness statements. At the station, while waiting to give their statements, both Lesley and Lisa are sitting close to that female passenger of the gold Mercedes. She has long brown hair and is covered in blood after attempting to revive her boyfriend at the scene.

"We were just relaying our story," Lesley says. "We didn't know the victim or his girlfriend. We didn't know anything about them."

Lisa overhears somebody say the victim's parents are from the Midwest and need to be contacted.

In the weeks that follow, detectives contact Lesley and the other women a few times with follow-up questions. They also send a sketch artist out to Merisel Inc. to get a physical description from Lesley.

The women hear nothing more about the murder until Jan. 6, 1996, when that sketch artist's same drawing, as well as a recording of Lesley's 911 call, appear on an episode of the popular "America's Most Wanted: America Fights Back." The hunt for a fugitive named Anthony Kuchta, a cocaine trafficker from Michigan who is still at large to this day, is the lead story on the episode before host John Walsh asks for tips in connection to the murder of a young man in Hollywood named Michael Nigg.

"I remember thinking it was crazy that case made America's Most Wanted," Lisa says.

The five women continue on with their lives without any more news of that horrible shooting in the parking lot behind The Art Store. Based on the number of eye witnesses and the description of the car, including a partial license plate, Lesley figures the killers will be caught eventually and justice will be served.

Almost three decades later, there is still no resolution.

"I just can't believe that they couldn't find them," Lesley says. "It's just insane to me."

In May, 2023, I send Lisa a Facebook message. She is surprised when I ask if she was a witness of a homicide in Hollywood in 1995. She does not know why I make a reference to O.J. Simpson — unaware that Michael Nigg once worked with Ronald Goldman, one of the most recognized murder victims of all time. She is also unaware that some conspiracy theorists out there have attempted to create a connection between the two murder cases.

Lisa points out that Lesley is her sister who was going by her married name at the time of the killing. She asks if I want to interview both of them at the same time during a conference call. Of course I do. After all, Lesley is the one who gets a good look at one of the suspects.

During the conference call, when I ask for Lesley's take on the conspiracy theories, she is quick to point out that Michael Nigg was not the suspects' first target that night.

"I have no doubt there is zero connection because of the way things went down," Lesley says. "It was just an opportunity that presented itself. They weren't lying in wait for that other car knowing they were coming."

Added Lisa, "If that other car doesn't show up, they would have been on us."

Not long after the conference call starts, I realize that both Lesley and Lisa are oblivious to what might be the most important fact of all.

"Ladies, are you aware that police arrested three suspects and later released them due to lack of evidence?"

There is a short pause before Lesley and Lisa answer almost simultaneously.

"No."

Adds Lisa, "One would think they would ask Lesley to see if she could recognize them."

Once again, a potential eyewitness never gets a look at photos of suspects police believe were the killers. In fact, police were so convinced, they appeal the district attorney's decision to set them free. Ironically, one of the reasons offered by the district attorney is the lack of a strong eyewitness.

Then, as I am speaking to Lesley, I realize that I am in possession of the suspects' mug shots.

"Lesley, would you like to see them?"

"See what?"

"The photos of the suspects. I have them."

"Yes. If you could email them to me, that would be great."

Within minutes, I attach photos of the suspects to an email and hit send. Immediately, I realize that I could be on the brink of a major development. Is Lesley Mobbs about to make a positive identification in the unsolved cold case of Michael Nigg's murder? She got a "good look" at the first suspect walking towards her – the suspect police believe was most likely the actual shooter.

Nineteen minutes later, I receive an email back from Lesley:

"Hi Brian. These are not the men I saw. The two men were black."

I point out that the men, who are brothers, are actually of Egyptian descent, but Lesley is not changing her mind.

I can't help but wonder if the results would be different if Lesley was shown the suspect photos at the time of the arrest. I also wonder how many other missed opportunities are out there.

If Lesley is correct, and these former suspects are not the killers, who murdered Michael Nigg?

CHAPTER 9 – THE INVESTIGATION

At 10:44 p.m. on Sept. 8, 1995, LAPD starts receiving a flurry of 911 calls to report a shooting behind The Art Store near Beverly Boulevard and Poinsettia Place in Hollywood. Two officers from the Wilshire area, identified as L. Perez and M. Pedroza, are first to arrive at the scene about five minutes later.

Citizens direct the officers to a wounded victim lying on his back between two vehicles in the parking lot, and an ambulance with the Los Angeles Fire Department arrives moments later. The officers secure the scene and request additional units to establish a perimeter.

The victim, identified as 26-year-old Michael Nigg, is wearing a blue Levi shirt and blue jeans. Nigg is transported to Cedars-Sinai Medical Center, where he is pronounced dead at 11:17 p.m. with a gunshot wound to the head.

I have photos of Michael at the crime scene, but I have decided not to include them in this book. I believe that would only cause more unnecessary pain for Michael's loved ones nearly three decades after the fact. However, I can tell you that seeing these photos for the first time really pisses me off. I keep remembering we were about the same age at the time of this shooting. I went to Hollywood often in the mid-1990s to hang out in restaurants and clubs on Friday nights. That could have been me lying there. I need to finish this book, and I need somebody with information to find it and read it. I really hate that Michael's killers are getting away with this.

Meanwhile, at 11 p.m., the Hollywood Area Watch Commander, Lt. M. Savala, sends two detectives from the station to the crime scene to provide guidance until the assigned investigators arrive. At 11:15 p.m., Savala contacts two on-call detectives with Hollywood Area Homicide — Tom Chevolek and Lloyd Parry — and assigns them to the case. They arrive at the crime scene just after 1 a.m.

Prior to their arrival, one of the first responders, identified as Officer Bowman, makes an incorrect guess when he sees a woman's purse on the street corner near the front of the The Art Store. Bowman assumes the purse, found 30-40 yards away from the shooting, must belong to Julie Long, the victim's girlfriend, and gives it to a detective.

It is not Julie's purse.

It does not take long for the detectives to find several pieces of evidence at the crime scene, including:

- A 9-mm cartridge case a few feet behind the right rear of the white Isuzu parked next to Julie's car.

- A round-nosed copper jacketed projectile found underneath a 1989 Saab parked in front of the Izuzu – about 15 feet away from the shooting.

- A green, blue and red sweater lying on the parkway on the northeast corner of the parking lot.

- An inverted, blood-smeared latex glove found a little north of the sweater in the middle of the Poinsettia.

- A cigarette butt as well as a partial tire tread just south of the driveway at 326 N. Poinsettia Place, across the street from the parking lot.

Julie Long's gold Mercedes Benz is impounded at Hollywood Tow until it can be dusted for fingerprints. Of the 23 prints lifted from the vehicle, 22 belong to Michael Nigg. One unidentified print is not clear enough to compare with others in the FBI's national database known as AFIS (Automated Fingerprint Identification System).

Police do not find any money on Michael, so they presume the $40 he just pulled from a nearby ATM must be with his killers. However, when Michael's best friend, Jay Spence, and roommate, Roberto Suelett, pull Julie's vehicle out of impound several days later, they find Michael's wallet on the back seat. Inside are two crisp $20 bills.

In other words, in return for Michael's life, it appears that his killers get nothing.

Detectives continue examining the crime scene until about 4:50 a.m., then return to the police station, where they begin searching through the purse recovered by Officer Bowman.

There is no wallet or money inside, but detectives do find some papers that indicate the purse belongs to a woman named Stacy Bartell. Detective Parry contacts Bartell, who reports that she was the victim of a purse snatching at about 10 p.m. on Sept. 8 in the 800 block of Gardner Street near Melrose Avenue.

Detectives quickly realize the purse snatching takes place 40 minutes prior to Michael Nigg's murder about a mile away. They call Bartell down to the station, where she informs detectives that her wallet, identification, credit cards and money are all missing from the purse. The investigators return the purse to Bartell.

The purse is never booked into evidence. Never tested for DNA.

News of another nearby incident a few hours after Michael's murder also begins to surface. At about 12:50 a.m., 22-year-old Kathryn Bisel is asleep in her apartment at 724 ½ N. Edinburgh Ave. – less than 1.5 miles from the shooting. Bisel wakes up to find three adult Black males – each armed with a semi-automatic pistol – demanding to know where "Henry" and the "money" are. When Bisel tells the suspects she does not know, one of the suspects says, "let's go," and grabs Bisel's camcorder as they walk out.

Outside, Bisel's boyfriend, identified as Henry Gray, comes home and observes three adult Black males walking out the front of the apartment complex. They enter a white sedan parked across the street. As Henry parks his car, a silver/blue Chevrolet Caprice sedan stops alongside him. The driver, a short-haired Black male, has a flip phone up to his ear and says, "What's up, Henry?"

Henry responds, "What's up?" He then hears the driver ask a question to whoever is on the other end of the phone. "Does he drive a blue Cabriolet convertible?"

At that moment, the high beams on the white sedan across the street light up before the vehicle speeds away. Gray attempts to pursue the white sedan, but he cannot keep pace as the vehicle runs several stop signs before reaching Santa Monica Boulevard.

Almost 30 years later, I am able to locate Henry Gray on social media. He accepts my friend request, but he does not respond to any of my messages. Did Henry Gray, who still lives in Los Angeles, know these men? If so, maybe they are also involved in Michael's murder . . . and/or Stacy's purse snatching.

Shortly after interviewing Kathryn Bisel and Henry Gray, the detectives contact one of the paramedics who worked the Michael Nigg crime scene. The paramedic, from LAFD Station 61, says he may have lost a glove as the ambulance carrying Michael took off northbound on Poinsettia Place.

After interviewing several witnesses, the detectives have a description on two of the three suspects.

- Presumed shooter – Black male, about 5 feet 10 inches in height, lean, early 20s in age, curly hair, light complexion, clean-shaven.

- Presumed lookout – Black male, about 6-1 or 6-2, lean, early 20s, short hair, light complexion, clean-shaven, wearing a white T-shirt.

Nobody appears to get a good look at the getaway driver. However, the getaway vehicle is described as a white sedan with a sunroof and an oblong-shaped emblem on the top center of the front grill.

Four days after the murder, Dana Bilvado, one of five co-workers sitting in a white Isuzu Trooper at the time of the shooting, sits down with a forensic artist to create a composite drawing of each of the suspects. Detectives then show the completed drawings to at least six other potential witnesses who offer their input. Patrol and gang officers throughout LAPD soon receive a copy of the composite drawings on 3x5 cards.

The detectives also sit down with Esther Adler, a 59-year-old woman who lives across the street from the parking lot at 330 N. Poinsettia Place. Esther gets a good look at the getaway car as the suspects flee the crime scene. Detectives show her various vehicle brochures, and she narrows her choices down to a 1994 Ford Taurus. She insists the vehicle has a sunroof.

In 2022, my fiancé and I decide to drive to Los Angeles to get a look at the crime scene. I park my Chevy Malibu in the same stall where Michael did. I look across the street and wonder if Esther still lives there. When I knock on the door, her son answers and informs me that Esther passed away several years earlier.

Detectives also learn about a purse snatching similar to Stacy's story that takes place on Aug. 2, 1995 – a little over a month before Michael's murder. At about 5:40 a.m., a 47-year-old woman is walking southbound in the 700 block of N. Hayworth Ave. when two adult Black males approach from the opposite direction. The suspects give the woman no choice but to walk between them. As they cross paths, one suspect grabs her purse, breaking the strap. The suspects run to a white compact sedan, driven by a third suspect, and it speeds away towards Melrose Avenue. It just so happens that Michael Nigg lives in an apartment at 741 N. Hayworth Ave. at the time of this robbery.

The cold case report does not include the name of the victim in this other purse snatching. Knowing that Stacy was never shown photos of arrested suspects until just a few years ago, I cannot help but doubt if this victim is given an opportunity.

On Sept. 27, 1995, a Hollywood gang officer contacts the detectives with a lead on a School Yard Crip gang member in jail who might have relevant information. Michael Xavier Terry tells detectives about three of his homies who were committing street robberies in the Hollywood area, including one near Poinsettia Place and Beverly Boulevard where the suspects got away with no money.

Detectives Parry and Chevolek interview Terry in county jail where he is in custody for an unrelated offense. When they inform Terry they are investigating the Michael Nigg case, Terry replies, "It wasn't right what they did to him."

Terry tells the detectives that he receives a visit from two fellow gang members, "JC and Lil' J Stone," sometime in mid-September asking to borrow a firearm. At the time, Terry is living in a Hollywood apartment with his 15-year-old girlfriend, Chrystal. Detectives already know that Terry's own moniker is "Lil' J Stone," so his story is already sketchy.

JC returns five days later with two other gang members, "Peanut and Baby Woody," and a story about a "jacking," or robbery. Terry says the new arrivals are acting paranoid and peeking out through the curtains because they "tried to jack a guy on Beverly and Poinsettia." When the victim refused, Peanut shot him in the head. When JC concludes his story, he hides a 9-mm pistol under Terry's sofa. The three men leave, Terry says, in an older white Buick Regal.

Terry tells detectives he is able to retrieve the murder weapon, but he refuses to reveal its location. Instead, he promises to contact a friend who will surrender the pistol to the detectives.

On Jan. 9, 1996, another jailhouse informant tells detectives he knows Michael Terry and two of his closest associates who are brothers, also known as "The Twins." He also recalls that Terry was in possession of a blue steel 9-mm pistol in August, 1995.

Later that month, detectives interview Terry's girlfriend, Chrystal Vigil. When detectives ask Vigil about Terry's closest associates, she mentions three people who are not gang members, but they like to rob people. Two of the men, Vigil says, are brothers of Cuban or Puerto Rican heritage who speak with a "Black accent." Their names are Mike and Steve, also known as "The Twins." She identifies the third person as Larry, a lifelong friend of Michael Terry.

When asked if she knows specifics about any of the street robberies, Vigil recalls "Mike, Steve and Larry" coming to the apartment at about 1 a.m. one evening and waking her up. Once inside, a stuttering Mike says, "We jacked some stupid ass mother fucker! The guy was stupid and scared. You should have seen his face!" Vigil tells Michael Terry she never heard Mike stutter like that before. Vigil also remembers Mike handing her boyfriend and "unknown object," and Terry placing it in a hiding spot behind the dresser.

Using department resources, detectives identify three suspects:

- Michael "Mike" Guirguis – Mid-east Arab, 6-3, 160 pounds, age 18.

- Steven "Steve" Guirguis – Mid-east Arab, 5-9, 135 pounds, age 19.

- Lawrence "Larry" Gardner – Black, 5-5, 120 pounds, age 20.

Detectives learn that the three men were arrested, along with two other Black males, for robbery in West Hollywood on Oct. 15, 1995, a little more than a month after Michael's murder. On that night, LA County Sherriff's deputies in an unmarked vehicle are stopped at a traffic light behind a brown 1980 Cadillac coupe at the corner of Santa Monica Boulevard and Orange Drive. Occupants of the vehicle are talking to several pedestrians standing on the corner when somebody inside appears to point a stainless steel pistol outside the passenger side window. They pull the vehicle over and order the occupants out at gunpoint. When they search the vehicle, they find an air pistol that resembles a .45 caliber pistol, two radio scanners, a wristwatch and a personal electronic organizer.

Steve Guirguis, the driver, tells deputies that he brandished the air pistol after the pedestrians on the corner started "talking shit." Mike Guirguis, the front passenger, says his brother was driving him home and did not know owned the recovered items. Larry Gardner says the group was out looking for a party. He has a nylon stocking – possibly a mask – in his right rear pants pocket. The other two occupants in the back seat say they do not know anything about an air pistol or the other items found.

Deputies arrest Steve Guirguis for brandishing a replica firearm. The four passengers are arrested and booked for probable cause robbery. They are later released for lack of evidence. The district attorney also declines to prosecute Steve Guirguis.

Deputies learn the electronic organizer belongs to a woman named Elizabeth Wang, who says her purse, containing the organizer, wallet, ID and $500 in cash, were stolen from beneath her chair while eating at a restaurant. She never reports the theft to police.

Detectives show booking photos of Mike and Steve Guirguis, and Larry Gardner, to Chrystal Vigil, who confirms they are the same three men who came to her apartment after 1 a.m. talking about a shooting somebody at Beverly Boulevard and Poinsettia Place.

I conduct a web search on Chrystal Dawn Vigil, and discover an LA Times article from Oct. 8, 1999 about the fatal shooting of a cab driver in Hollywood. The article states that police have arrested two women in the shooting, but Vigil remains at large. Vigil is 19 when this article is published, so she would be about the same age as Michael Terry's girlfriend. The popular TV show, "America's Most Wanted," later produces a segment about Vigil and the cab driver. From what I could find on the web, Vigil is captured in 2006.

In 2022, I am able to track down Chrystal Dawn Vigil living in Kokomo, Indiana. She confirms that she is the same person whom detectives interviewed in the Michael Nigg murder case, but she does not wish to be interviewed out of fear of Michael Xavier Terry. After the phone call, I realize I forgot to ask if she is the former fugitive in the cab driver murder, so I send her a text. I am never able to locate Michael Xavier Terry.

"I pray you are able able to find justice but I gave you all I know. (Terry) is a very scary man and I want nothing to do with him . . . "

At 6:45 a.m. on Feb. 8, 1996, police are outside the Guirguis residence preparing to execute a search warrant when "The Twins" walk out. They are immediately taken into custody for the murder of Michael Nigg.

Fifteen minutes later, a second team executes a warrant at Larry Gardner's residence. Gardner is not there, but police do seize some narcotics paraphernalia. Michael Guirguis directs police to another address, where Gardner voluntarily comes outside and is quickly arrested for Michael's murder. The house belongs to Anthony Wyatt, one of the other passengers in the vehicle at the corner on Oct. 15, 1995.

Wyatt denies any knowledge of the Nigg murder when interviewed by police, but he says "The Twins" often boasted about having "jacked" people.

Detectives show photos of the three arrestees to all but one of the Nigg eyewitnesses. Susan Westcott says she is

100 percent confident that Michael Guirguis is one of the suspects she saw while walking back to her car. None of the other witnesses, however, are able to make a positive identification.

In an interview with detectives, Michael Guirguis at first denies having knowledge of any street robberies, but later admists that his brother, Steve, and Gardner were committing purse snatches. He denies any knowledge of the Nigg murder, however, before he is booked at Hollywood Jail.

Before detectives complete their interviews, Terry calls from jail to say he is ready to spill his guts. He confirms that Peanut, JC and Baby Woody are indeed Gardner and "The Twins." He says that when the suspects came to his house in the early hours of Sept. 9, 1995, Larry tells him that Mike is the actual shooter. Terry also says they also were driving a white coupe with a sunroof that evening.

During his interview, Gardner acknowledges a close association with "The Twins," as well as their frequent visits to Terry's apartment. He denies any knowledge of Michael Nigg's murder or making any statements to Terry's girl-friend, Chrystal.

Steve Guirguis also denies any involvement in Nigg's murder, and claims he has not been to Terry's apartment in over a year. When told of reports that he was bragging about the murder in Terry's apartment, Steve tells detectives that he was "only bullshitting." Four days later, when detectives try for a second interview, Steve asks for an attorney.

Larry Gardner, on the other hand, agrees to a polygraph test. During the examination, he actually admits to participating in the Nigg robbery-homicide. Detectives Parry and Chevolek want another interview. Gardner says Steve parked his brown Cadillac on a residential side street just off a busy roadway after "The Twins" said the needed money.

Less than a minute later, a gold vehicle enters the parking lot. "The Twins" say they are going to "jack" it since the occupants were likely to have money. Steve and Michael approach the gold car on foot, and then Steve confronts the male victim at the open driver's door. By this time, Gardner is standing outside the vehicle. Gardner says he sees Mike step forward to assist his brother before stepping back and firing one shot. "The Twins" run back to the vehicle, and they drive to Michael Terry's apartment. Detectives never ask Gardner about the purse snatching of Stacy Bartell.

On Feb. 12, 1996, Gardner calls detectives from the jail saying he wants to talk. When detectives arrive, Gardner claims he made up the confession and now wants an attorney.

Later that day, detectives present their information to Los Angeles County Deputy District Attorney Robert Savitt, who says he will have a decision the next day on whether or not to press charges. The next day, Savitt declines prosecution pending further investigation. He wants to know if blood on the latex glove found near the scene is human and if any fingerprints can be lifted from inside the glove.

Detectives come back quickly with confirmation that the blood is human, but they are unable to develop any prints. Two days later, Savitt declines prosecution again for a number of reasons, including:

- Julie Long, along with several other witnesses can not identify the suspects.

- Michael Terry is a convicted felon currently in state prison. He is also a potential accomplice if he indeed hid the murder weapon.

- Lack of physical evidence.

- Although he is allegedly aware of the robbery plan, Gardner himself does not actively participate.

- Chrystal Vigil's age and relationship to Michael Terry.

However, detectives believe strongly they have their suspects, and they appeal Savitt's decision to the supervising deputy district attorney, identified in the cold case report as G. Somes. Mr. Somes concurs with Savitt, citing the "dubious credibility" of the witnesses. Michael and Steve Guirguis, and Larry Gardner, are released.

Twenty-eight years later, I am able to find some social media pages for all three of the former suspects. However, I am unable to make a connection. I would especially like to hear from Mr. Gardner on the circumstances that led to his "confession." Was he really involved, or was he somehow coerced into admitting his involvement? Was he promised leniency in exchange for his cooperation?

Around this same time, in 1995, 18-year-old Gerardo Cabanillas confesses to his involvement in a robbery of a couple sitting in a parked car in South Gate. The man is forced out of the car, and the woman is taken to an abandoned house and raped by two men. Thanks to his "confession," Cabanillas is convicted a year later and spends 28 years in prison. He is released in 2023 after DNA testing exonerates him.

During a press conference, as Cabanillas is released from prison, the current Los Angeles County District Attorney, George Gascon, addresses what he describes as a "tragic miscarriage of justice."

"Mr. Cabanillas always maintained that on the date of his

arrest, he was coerced by the investigating detective into giving a false confession with a promise that he would be released on probation."

Nine months after Gardner and the Guirguis brothers are released, the Michael Nigg murder case is reclassified to "Cleared Other." It is among hundreds of murder cases that LAPD closes without actually solving. According to the Los Angeles Daily News, LAPD classified 596 homicides as "cleared other" from 2000 to 2010.

A cousin of one of those murder victims is not happy his case is closed without being solved.

"How is it closed when there's nobody in jail?" asks Jose Aguayo, whose cousin, Ernesto Cardena is shot to death in his driveway in Arleta in 2008. "My cousin is in a cemetery, but these guys are walking free."

Nine months after Michael Nigg's case is classified as "Cleared Other," the detectives and their superiors meet with Deputy District Attorney G. Knoke for one final appeal. Once again, they are denied due to the perceived lack of credibility of the witnesses.

Soon after, the case is archived and collects dust for the next 22 years until March 16, 2018, when a LAPD cold case detective named Scott Masterson receives a phone call from a woman named Stacy from Virginia.

CHAPTER 10 – VEGAS BOOMS!

It is 1:50 a.m. on Sunday, Sept. 19, 2010 in North Las Vegas near the corner of Craig and Pecos roads — just east of the Interstate 15 exit. Most of the businesses at this intersection are closed for the night, and most of the residents of a large neighborhood across the street are sound asleep in their beds. It is a quiet and peaceful desert evening with temperatures just below 70 degrees.

The main entrance to Nellis AFB, where the world famous Air Force Thunderbirds nest, is less than three miles to the east. If you drive north on Interstate 15 a few more exits, you will find Las Vegas Motor Speedway. The neon glow of the Las Vegas Strip is clearly visible about 12 miles to the south.

At 3826 E. Craig Road, employee Franklyn Hernandez is preparing to lock up Viva Zapata's! Mexican Restaurant & Cantina for the night. The popular restaurant pays tribute to Emiliano Zapata, who led a peasant uprising against greedy landowners during the Mexican Revolution of the early 1900s. Viva Zapatas! shares a parking lot with JCW Mini Mart, a financially struggling gas station and convenience store located right next door.

Suddenly, an explosion just outside the restaurant shakes

the ground below Franklyn's feet. He and his co-workers immediately run over to the front window and discover that the JCW Mini Mart has exploded into flames. They quickly exit the restaurant and reach a safe distance before Franklyn calls 911.

Meanwhile, about 450 miles northwest at the Lovelock Correctional Center, in Pershing County, Nev., Prisoner 1027820 is asleep in his cell. The 62-year-old by no means is your typical, ordinary inmate. He is O.J. Simpson, the man acquitted of the murders of Nicole Brown and Ronald Goldman in 1995 before somehow getting himself into all kinds of trouble again in the fall of 2007. That is when he and some of his cronies entered a room at the Palace Station hotel in Las Vegas and held a sports memorabilia collector at gunpoint. Simpson claimed he was only there to retrieve items he insisted belonged to him.

On Sept. 19, 2007, exactly three years before this explosion at the JCW Mini Mart, Simpson appeared before Justice of the Peace Joe Boneventure Jr. to hear a long list of felony charges against him, including armed robbery and kidnapping. Bail was set at $125,000. Less than a year later, a jury would find Simpson guilty and sentence him to 33 years in prison – much to the delight of many people on the planet who believe he got away with double murder 12 years earlier in Brentwood, Calif.

What does O.J. Simpson have to do with a gas station explosion in North Las Vegas? Nothing really . . . unless you begin to apply the seven degrees of Ronald Goldman . . .

. . . and friends.

Incorporated in 1946, The City of North Las Vegas offers the full range of municipal services for its 200,000-plus residents. When emergency dispatch receives a flood of 911 calls about an explosion and a fully involved fire at the JCW Mini Mart at 3820 E. Craig Road, police and fire crews arrive within just a few minutes. They discover smoldering debris scattered throughout the large parking lot. Forty firefighters extinguish the blaze in less than a half-hour, but the building is a total loss.

A TV news crew also arrives at the scene, but there is another incident happening at the same time about 13 miles away that is certain to attract more media attention than a gas station fire with no *apparent* injuries. At the Hard Rock Hotel, Las Vegas police are busy arresting singer/songwriter Bruno Mars for cocaine possession after a bathroom attendant spotted him coming out of a stall with a baggy of white nose candy.

Mars, who performed earlier at the hotel, is on the brink of stardom. His first single, "Just the Way You Are," is currently No. 3 on the Billboard Hot 100. His debut album, "Doo-Wops & Hooligans," is set for release in 15 days. He tells police he has never used drugs before (something he will later admit is a lie) before he is booked at the Clark County Detention Center under his real name – Peter Hernandez. A Clark County District Court judge will eventually dismiss the charges after Mars successfully completes drug education classes and community service.

Back in North Las Vegas, investigators are trying to figure out what happened at the JCW Mini-Mart. They start interviewing owners and employees of nearby businesses who are now at the scene.

Joseph Nocerino, owner of the Meineke Car Care Center, describes having a conversation the previous afternoon with a man named "Frenchy," who managed JCW Mini-Mart. He says Frenchy complained that the store was losing money, and that the fuel tanks were leaking. Nocerino adds that the store closed for good at about 3 p.m. the day before.

Nocerino's brother, Vincent, tells an investigator he spoke to a man named "Pete," the owner of the property, for the first time the previous day. He says Pete changed all the locks at the store, which Frenchy was renting from him.

Ryan Thompson, an employee at Village Shop No. 7, says he witnessed people moving belongings into a U-Haul truck at about 2 a.m. the previous morning. Also, three hours before the explosion, Thompson recalls seeing a pickup truck – a Chevy or GMC – parked in front of the store with its lights off.

One of the fire investigators, who asks to remain anonymous for this book, believes this was a combustion explosion. He rules out electricity as the cause of the explosion after discovering all the circuit breakers are in the "off" position. After looking at the meter readings, he also determines there was not enough natural gas used to produce an explosion of this magnitude.

When investigators move to the east end of the property, they discover a small storage closet between the gas station and an attached car wash. Inside the closet are three empty 1-gallon gas containers and one empty quart can of MEK (Methyl Ethyl Ketone), a highly flammable liquid used as a solvent for laquers, adhesives and cleaning products. They also find two black gas caps in a driveway between the gas station and Meineke Car Care Center.

Suspicion is already mounting even before investigators find an unlocked back door to the property. This fire is no accident. The authorities now have an arson investigation on their hands.

At 12:29 p.m. on Sunday, a 178-word article appears on

The Las Vegas Sun website. The headline reads, *"Explosion rocks gas station in North Las Vegas; no injuries."* The article states that the cause of the explosion and fire is under investigation. There is no mention of possible arson.

After searching for clues for nearly 12 hours on Sunday, investigators have a chain link fence installed around the entire property. It is double-chained and locked. A closer examination of the site will resume first thing Monday morning when it is safe to dig deeper into the charred debris.

In the meantime, one investigator is able to verify the property owner through the Clark County Assessor's Office. His name is Pete Argyris, who lives at 9948 Keifer Valley Street in Las Vegas. After several failed attempts to reach Argyris on his cell phone, Las Vegas police leave a contact card at his residence.

At about 2:30 p.m., the investigator finally gets a call back from Argyris. Some of his comments are included in the investigator's final report.

> *"Hello. I received a phone call from this number. Who is this?"*

After identifying himself, the investigator states the reason for his call. "We would like to talk to you about a fire at a building you own.

> *"I don't know anything about a fire. I had a long night out, and I am really hung over."*

The investigator explains that the fire is "significant," and his presence at the property is very important.

> *"I had a rather long night and I am very hung over,*

and at this time, it's not a priority for me. Can I call
you in the morning to make an appointment with
you?"

"Well, we would really like to talk to you today," the investigator responds, "but if that's not an option, tomorrow will have to work."

Before he hangs up, Argyris offers some info that catches the investigator off guard.

"Oh by the way, the person who was leasing the
building from me was selling bad gas to people and
made many enemies. I believe someone started the
fire with gasoline."

At 4:30 p.m., another investigator shows up at Argyris' front door on Keifer Valley Street. Argyris tells the investigator he is still hung over after a heavy night of partying. He says he wants to see the property, but it would be unsafe for him to drive. The investigator asks Argyris to explain what is going on.

Argyris continues the process of throwing Frenchy – later identified as Philippe Jean Savignard of Las Vegas — under the bus. He accuses Frenchy of selling bad gas, leading to many broken vehicles and angry customers. He says the business is failing, and Frenchy is behind on his rent of $14,100 per month. Argyris adds that Frenchy removed all merchandise and appliances from the gas station in recent days, and he was concerned that Frenchy was going to remove the gas pumps at some point. For this reason, Argyris says he changed the locks on the doors.

Two hours later, a North Las Vegas police officer is talking to an employee at Viva Zapatas! about all the excitement from early that morning. The employee shares that he hurried out to the restaurant at 3 a.m. after receiving a phone call from a co-worker. When he arrived, he noticed a suspicious-looking vehicle parked behind the restaurant. He then points to a silver Chrysler Town and Country mini-van still parked in the exact same spot just 100 feet from the gas station.

As they walk over to the van, the officer asks the employee why he thinks it looks suspicious. The employee explains that when he left work at 1 a.m., the van was not there. Two hours later when he returned, it was there.

All the doors to the mini-van are locked. The officer peers through one of the windows and notices at least two bottles of an unknown brand of alcohol. The third-row seats are folded forward to leave room for cargo, but no cargo is present. He also notices a folded-up bed sheet. A quick check with dispatch on the license plate reveals the mini-van belongs to Payless Car Rental.

The officer contacts one of the arson investigators and advises him about a rental van that might have parked near the gas station sometime between 1 and 3 a.m. that morning. The investigator believes he now has probable cause to link the rental van to a possible arson, so he has the vehicle towed away into custody.

The investigator then places a call to Payless Car Rental. An agent says the person who rented the mini-van is a woman named Patricia Patterson. Later that morning, at 6 a.m., an officer knocks on the front door at Patterson's address. Patterson explains that she rented a mini-van for her boyfriend, 26-year-old Brandon Davis. She also says she last spoke to Brandon at 1:30 a.m., which happens to be about 20 minutes prior to the explosion.

"... he told me he had some business that he had to take care of, and he would be right home," she tells the officer.

However, Davis still is not home, and Patterson has no idea where he is. She is worried sick.

About three hours later, back at the scene of the explosion, the search for physical evidence kicks into high gear. One of the arson investigators is carefully excavating the debris, working from the least amount of damage to the worst.

At this same moment, about eight miles south at the Clark County Regional Justice Center, another famous celebrity is in hot water after being arrested for cocaine possession a month earlier. Paris Hilton, the hotel heiress and reality show queen, is standing before Justice of the Peace Joe Bonaventure to receive her sentence on two misdemeanor charges. Bonaventure gives Hilton a year of probation, a $2,000 fine and 200 hours of community service, and he orders her to complete an intensive substance abuse program.

"I'm going to warn you, Miss Hilton, you've now been sentenced to one year in the Clark County Detention Center," Bonaventure says. "The Clark County Detention Center is not the Waldorf Astoria. But I assure you that if you violate the terms of your probation you will serve one year in the Clark County Detention Center. Treat this very seriously. Do you understand me?"

As Hilton takes her lumps, the arson investigator up north sifts through the debris. The sound of morning traffic along nearby Interstate 15 can be heard in the background. The investigator already has his suspicions based on witness interviews and physical evidence collected so far.

He moves towards the center of what is left of the

building. He carefully lifts up a large, metal HVAC manifold and discovers the badly-burned body of what appears to be an adult male. It is a surprise for fire officials who already told local media there were no injuries in the explosion.

The excavation work immediately stops, and North Las Vegas police detectives arrive a short time later. A special agent with the Bureau of Alcohol, Tobacco, Firearms and Explosives (ATF) also responds to the scene.

Big story? Apparently not. Later that afternoon, the Las Vegas Sun posts another short article on its web site. It is just a few paragraphs longer than Sunday's story. This headline reads, "Body Found in NLV gas station that exploded Sunday."

"It is too early to classify this case an anything more than a death investigation," police said in a statement.

Four days later, on Sept. 24, the Clark County Coroner's Office announces it has identified the body as 26-year-old Brandon Davis. Big story? Nope. The Las Vegas Sun posts a follow-up that is shorter than the previous two. There are no press conferences, no interviews with detectives, no digging by reporters, no comments from family or friends.

Oddly, Las Vegas media will not mention the name of Brandon Davis again for another four years, four months and 25 days.

Michael Nigg was murdered in this small parking lot behind The Art Store in Hollywood on the evening of Sept. 8, 1995.

A rare photo of Michael Nigg provided by former co-worker Marika Repasi.

Michael was standing inside the doorway of his girlfriend's gold Mercedes-Benz when armed robbers approached demanding money. When he refused, a scuffle ensued before one of the robbers shot Michael in the head.

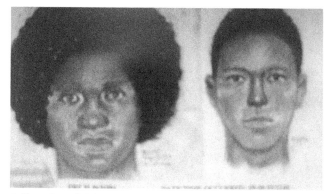

Police released this sketch of the suspects after interviewing several witnesses.

Pete Argyris and his mother, JoAnn Argyris.

Brandon Davis.

Brandon Davis used this gray rental van to carry out an arson that would ultimately take his own life in 2010.

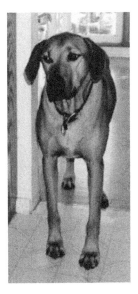

Zimba, a highly-trained Rhodesian Ridgeback, was a few feet away from Nicole just minutes before prosecutor Marcia Clark says she was murdered.

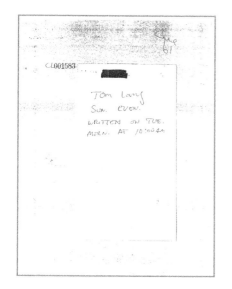

CL001583

Tom Lang
Sun. even.
Written on Tue.
morn. at 10:00 am

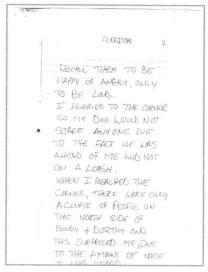

CL001590 2

recall them to be
happy or angry, only
to be loud.
I hurried to the corner
so my dog would not
scare anyone due
to the fact he was
ahead of me and not
on a leash.
When I reached the
corner, there were only
a couple of people on
the north side of
Bundy & Dorthy and
this surprized me; due
to the amount of noise
I had heard

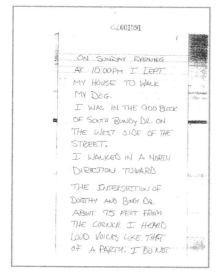

CL001591 1

On Sunday evening
at 10:00 pm I left
my house to walk
my dog.
I was in the 900 block
of South Bundy Dr. on
the west side of the
street.
I walked in a north
direction toward
the intersection of
Dorthy and Bundy Dr.
About 75 feet from
the corner I heard
loud voices like that
of a party. I do not

Tom Lang's 9-page handwritten statement delivered to District Attorney's office on the morning of June 14, 1994.

I WAS ABOUT TO
GIVE MY DOG THE
COMMAND TO CROSS WHEN
I FOUND I COULD NOT
SEE IF THE CARS COMING
SOUTH ON BUNDY WERE
GOING TO TURN RIGHT.
MY VIEW WAS BLOCKED
BY A WHITE FORD
TRUCK TYPE VECH..
IT WAS PARKED ON
THE WEST SIDE OF
BUNDY FACING SOUTH
NEAR THE LARGE TREE
ON THE CORNER.
I WAITED FOR THE
CARS TO PASS THEN

VOICE COMMAND SHE
LOOKED AT ME THEN
AT THE DOG THEN
BACK TOWARD BUNDY
AT THE TRUCK PARKED
THERE. (SHE WAS
MED. HT. - BLOND -
IN DARK CLOTHING.)
I COULD NOT SEE WHO
WAS STANDING ON
THE PASS. SIDE OF
THE TRUCK BECAUSE
THE DOOR WAS HALF
OPEN AND THE TREE
WAS BLOCKING MY VIEW.
I THEN ALSO HEADED

4

HEADED NORTH, CROSSING
DORTHY.
AT 3/4 OF THE WAY
ACROSS THE STREET I
WAS FORCED TO GIVE
MY DOG A VERBAL AND
HAND COMMAND TO HEAD
WEST ON THE SIDEWALK
TOWARD GRETNA GREEN.
HE WAS HEADING BEFORE
MY COMMAND TOWARDS A
TREE AT THE CORNER
AND THERE WAS A LADY
STANDING ON THE PARK-
WAY BY THE TREE.
WHEN I SAID THE

Tom Lang's 9-page handwritten statement (continued)

WEST ON THE SIDE-
WALK ALONG DORTHY
TOWARD GRETNA GREEN
BUT FIRST LOOKED
NORTH - UP THE SIDE-
WALK ALONG BUNDY
ABOUT 40-50 FT UP
WAS A MAN. (HE
WAS AROUND MY SIZE
5'11" '75 - WHITE.)
HE HAD ON DARK
CLOTHING. HE ALSO HAD
A RIDGED POSTURE. WITH
HIS FIST CLENCHED.
HE DID NOT SPEAK BUT
STOOD STOPED. I HAD THOUGH
MY DOG HAD SCARED

HIM. I THEN
PROCEEDED WEST TO
GRETNA GREEN THEN
BACK ACROSS DORTHY
SOUTH TOWARD MAYFAIR
EAST TO BUNDY AND
NORTH HOME

I CAN NOT REMEMBER
HEARING ANY TALKING
AFTER THE FIRST LOUD
VOICES.
I WOULD HAVE TO SAY
THE FEMALE I SAW WAS
NOT HAPPY AND LOOKED MAD.
THE MAN ON THE SIDEWALK
WAS TO FAR AWAY TO SEE

FACIAL EXP.
I DID NOT EVER
SEE THE PERSON
AT THE TRUCK CLEH.
ENOUGH TO TELL ANYTH

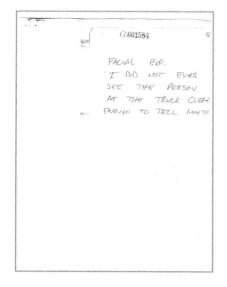

Tom Lang's 9-page handwritten statement (continued)

CHAPTER 11 – PETE AND HIS MOM

As I continue scanning through Kim Goldman's civil trial deposition on Feb. 5, 1996, attorney Philip Baker asks Ron's sister for one of the answers I am looking for.

Q. Who was Ron's best friend?

A. Mike Pincus and Pete Argyris.

Q. Mike Pincus, how do you spell that name?

A. P-i-n-c-u-s.

Q. Where does he live?

A. Thousand Oaks.

Q. Do you know his phone number?

A. I would be guessing.

Q. Why don't you give me your guess, if you have any idea.

A. [Number deleted.]

Q. What is the second one?

A. Pete Argyris.

Q. How do you spell that?

A. A-r-g-y-r-i-s.

Q. Where does he live?

A. Las Vegas.

Is there any chance these guys would be willing to talk to me about the *real* Ron Goldman? I suppose it does not hurt to try. Heck, they might even know something about what Ron was driving that night.

I immediately start searching in social media for Mike Pincus, and I find a page called "Mike Pincus Fitness Podcast." Kim identifies Mike as a fitness trainer in 1996, so there is a good chance this is my guy. I send him a short message to introduce myself and politely ask for an interview. It doesn't take long to get a response.

> *"Hi Brian, it depends on what you are interested in talking about regarding Ron Goldman."*

I tell Mr. Pincus I am trying to find out more about Ron as well as Mike Nigg.

> *"For what reason if you don't mind me asking? Who's Mike Nigg?"*

At this point in my journey, I am still in discovery myself when it comes to Michael Nigg. I have not received the full report from Detective Masterson, so I have not yet landed on the other side of the moon. I explain, as best as I can, how Michael was murdered during the criminal trial, and how the case remains unsolved.

> *"I don't know Mike Nigg. But that doesn't mean he didn't know Ron. Yes I knew Ron. But I would need to know more about the book and the angle of the book."*

Honestly, at this point I really don't know how to answer him.

"It would be very difficult to say what the angle is because I'm just gathering content now. However, I can say I'm exploring their relationship and the possibility their murders might be related. You are identified as one of Ron's two best friends. . . That's why I reached out."

> *"I can guarantee you this, there is no relationship between these two murders! I have no idea who killed Mike Nigg. But O.J. definitely killed Ron!"*

I try to keep it somewhat friendly because I do not want him to shut down.

"I appreciate your passion dude. Look . . . if you change your mind. . . or maybe if you're willing to go off the record . . . let me know. Can I ask you one more thing? Were you friends with Pete Argyris?"

Mike Pincus never responds after that. If I had read the Goldman family's book, "His Name is Ron," ahead of time, I would have appreciated how good of a best friend Mike Pincus really was. During Ron's funeral, Pincus delivers one of the most heartwarming speeches you can imagine. At the time, Pincus and his wife are expecting a baby in three months.

"He would have made a great Uncle Ron," Pincus says.

Well, one best friend down . . . one best friend to go. I go back to social media and begin a search for Pete Argyris. I find nothing. Since Kim has given me a hometown for Pete, I decide on a Google search: "Pete Argyris Las Vegas."

Another bizarre journey is about to begin.

At the top of the Google page is a press release from the U.S. Department of Justice of all places. The headline reads, "Las Vegas Business Man And His Mother Charged With Arson For 2010 Convenience Store Fire In Which Man Died." It is dated Feb. 18, 2015.

> *"LAS VEGAS, Nev. – A Las Vegas man and his mother have been indicted by the federal grand jury on charges that they destroyed the mini-mart they owned in North Las Vegas in order to collect the insurance proceeds, announced U.S. Attorney Daniel G. Bogden for the District of Nevada.*
>
> *Pete Argyris, 46, of Las Vegas, and his mother, Joann Argyris, 67, of Boulder City, Nev., are charged with conspiracy to commit arson, arson resulting in death, use of fire to commit mail fraud, six counts of mail fraud, and criminal forfeiture. They were arrested yesterday evening by ATF Special Agents, and are scheduled for arraignment and plea at 3 p.m. today before U.S. Magistrate Judge George Foley, Jr. If convicted, they face up to life in prison on the conspiracy and arson charges, 10 years consecutive on the use of fire to commit*

mail fraud charge, up to 20 years in prison on each
mail fraud charge, and fines of up to $250,000 on
each count."

Pause. Pause. Pause. Holy crap. Arson resulting in death? Life in prison?

Is it possible this is the same Pete Argyris? Ron Goldman's best friend? Well, I do a little math, and if he is 46 in 2015, that puts him in his mid-20s at the time of Ron's murder. How many people with a name like Pete Argyris, with the right age, live in the same place. I have to keep digging.

One would think this kind of story is big news. However, both The Las Vegas Sun and The Review Journal essentially produce re-writes of the DOJ press release. There does not appear to be any independent reporting involved in either.

My thoughts at this moment are all over the place. Is one of Ron Goldman's best friends sitting in a federal prison cell somewhere? Ft. Leavenworth? This is just crazy. There has to be some stories about Pete and his mom on trial somewhere, right? Does a jury find them guilty? What are their sentences? The press release also offers the name of a fatal victim – 26-year-old Brandon Davis. What is his story?

Even more bizarre than finding this press release is the fact that I cannot find any more after it. There is nothing related to the fate of Pete and his mom on the web. The press release is almost a decade old. There has to be something more to this story.

Once again, I find myself forgetting about Ron Goldman, and in complete wonder about yet another topic on the flip side of O.J.'s moon. How many other strange stories like this exist out here?

Well, what now? At the bottom of that original DOJ press release is the name of Assistant U.S. Attorney Phillip N. Smith, Jr., who is identified as the prosecutor. I call a phone number at the bottom of the web site, and it is no longer in service. I do a Google search for Smith and find a person of the same name in private practice in Las Vegas. I figure it must be him. I call the number on his web site, and a man answers the phone immediately. It is none other than Phillip Smith. I introduce myself and ask him if he recalls a case in 2015 involving Pete Argyris and his mother.

"I do remember the case, but it was such a long time ago," Smith says. "You really need to talk to the arson investigator in North Las Vegas."

Smith gives me a name, which isn't hard to find on the web. I find a phone number and leave a message, then another. On the third try, the investigator answers. I give him the same introduction and inquiry I gave Smith. This response is much different.

"Ohhhhhhh man. I can tell you everything you want to know about that guy."

Now we're talking! When I explain that I am all ears, he offers a better suggestion.

"You should probably just come out here."

This is exciting. I am about to make my first road trip for this book project. We agree to meet on a Saturday morning in his office. I bring my oldest daughter with me for company. She loves true crime stuff.

I shake hands with the investigator in the parking lot, and he unlocks the front door to the Fire Administration Building in North Las Vegas. We head upstairs, and sit down in his office. After some brief chitchat about his background, he says, "Why don't you come with me?"

We walk down the hallway to a very small room that looks more like a large closet. He flips on the light and points to the wall.

"That is the Pete Argyris case."

The entire wall reminds me of a scene out of a movie. There are dozens of photos of suspects and witnesses, all kinds of notes, and a spaghetti of yarn connecting everything together. It is so strange that I am even standing here. I immediately walk over to the wall with my legal pad ready to write as fast as I can.

"Here, let me help you."

The investigator starts taking everything off the wall. I mean everything. We walk downstairs to a copy machine, and he begins scanning every item to his computer back in his office. We walk upstairs, and he loads all the files to a flash drive.

"OK, I am going to give this to you, but I don't want to be quoted," he says. "Deal?"

In my days as a reporter, that is not something I normally would agree to except for extreme situations where there is no alternative. Publishers and editors do not like anonymous sources, but this is information I cannot live without.

"Deal."

Before I leave, I have two big questions to ask the investigator. The first thing I hope to find out is if Ron Goldman's name ever came up during his investigation.

"Ron Goldman? You mean, like Ron Goldman from the OJ case?"

"Yes, I think there is a really strong chance your guy was one of Ron Goldman's closest friends."

"Oh. Wow. I thought I knew everything about Pete Argyris. That is news to me."

The second question I have is the most important. Where is Pete?

I need to know what happened to Pete Argyris. Does he go to trial with his mother? Is he sitting in a prison cell somewhere for the rest of his life? If so, he maybe I can get an interview. Maybe Pete is willing to talk candidly about Ron Goldman's life behind the scenes. What does he have to lose? Then again, maybe he has already served a lighter sentence and is moving on with his life. The investigator gives me an answer I am not expecting.

"Pete is dead."

Wait. What? My daughter and I give each other a confused look before I ask the investigator for a little more.

"He overdosed on cocaine right before the trial started."

The "C" word has returned. The investigator explains that Pete Argyris was a major coke addict. He loved to party. He loved the Vegas nightlife, and that ultimately led to his downfall.

And the mom?

"I'm not really sure. I think she ended up getting probation."

I am sure you can imagine the conversation with my daughter on our three-hour drive home. One thing I do know. I cannot wait to plug that flash drive into my computer.

As I open all these files, it is very apparent that the case of Pete Argyris and his mother is worthy of its own book. It certainly deserves more media attention than it received. As I read the arson investigator's report, as well as all the witness statements, it does appear the investigator is right about Pete's downward spiral into financial desperation.

According to the charges, Pete, who runs a fitness center in nearby Henderson, pays one of his employees, Brandon Davis, to set one of his failing businesses, the JCW Mini-Mart in North Las Vegas, on fire on Sept. 19, 2010. Even though he is under suspicion by the authorities, Pete later submits an insurance claim seeking $1.4 million. The mother is suspected of having some knowledge of the fraud scheme, but the extent of her involvement is unclear to me so far.

I begin digging into the case, which quickly starts to feel like a rabbit hole I might not ever return from. I start looking for witnesses on social media. One of them is a woman named Kristine Mraz, who is Pete's former girlfriend still living in Las Vegas. I send her a message, asking if I can interview her for a book project related to the O.J. murder case.

"Why me?"

I explain to Kristine that I recently learned about Pete Argyris, including the gas station explosion, the overdose, etc., and I am curious if Pete ever relayed any information to her about Ron Goldman. She offers to tell me what she knows, "but I don't think it's that great of info."

I ask Kristine if Pete ever shared anything about his relationship with Ron, how they met, what they did together, etc. I ask if Pete ever shared his thoughts about the murders. I ask if Pete ever mentioned doing any drugs with Ron. Then it occurs to me . . . if Pete knew Ron, and Ron knew Michael Nigg, maybe Pete knew Michael Nigg.

At first, Michael Nigg's name does not sound familiar to Kristine, then I receive a message from her about an hour later.

"I believe I know of Michael Nigg. My old roommate Julie Mills dated him. She was there in her car when he was murdered. Someone approached the car while he was getting out to let Julie out of the car."

Pause. Pause. Pause. Oh my. Let me get this straight. Sometime after Michael Nigg's murder, Julie Long (now Julie Mills) moves to Las Vegas and becomes the roommate of Pete's ex-girlfriend? Seriously, what are the chances? What Kristine does not realize at this moment is that I now have a lead on Julie. I will later discover that, in 1997, Julie marries actor Judson Mills, best known for his work as Chuck Norris' sidekick on *Walker, Texas Ranger*. The couple divorces in 2002 before Julie moves to Las Vegas and meets Kristine through a mutual friend.

"She was still very hurt by his death," Kristine says, referring to Michael.

Kristine, who begins dating Pete around 2006, suspects that Pete and Ron Goldman were not exactly besties.

"From what I remember of Pete talking about Ron, it wasn't much of a relationship . . . seemed more like casual friends. He said he met Ron at his tanning salon that he owned in Agoura Hills. Pete showed me some photos they took together on someone's patio drinking. I saw Ron in the background and he was looking away, so it was as if Ron wasn't really part of the photo, but who knows? Back then, there was always such candid pictures taken, not really posed or looking directly into the camera.

"Pete told me that Ron was a show off kind of guy and would boast about anyone he's dating, and Pete never heard of him dating or doing anything with Nicole. She was a beautiful older woman. Pete felt Ron would have been saying something about it."

Kristine also offers another interesting tidbit that I am unaware of at the time – that Pete Argyris was one of the pallbearers at Ron's funeral. I send her a stock photo from the web showing the pallbearers carrying the coffin. She sends it back with a circle around Pete.

"When I found out that Pete was one of the pallbearers, I was surprised. Pete didn't say he was his best friend but maybe did it because one of Ron's closer friends wasn't doing it, so he stepped in to support that friend."

Kristine also shares her thoughts about Pete's final days.

"He partied hard his whole life and I'm sure his criminal trial was wearing on him physically. It had just got postponed for like the seventh or eighth time. Then two weeks later after it was postponed, then he died, on a weekday morning. He was found by his mother when she unable to reach him."

I continue corresponding with Kristine several times over the next several days. In the meantime, I need to learn more about Pete's mom, and just when you think things can't get any crazier . . .

In 2005, JoAnn Argyris and her daughter stroll into the Railroad Pass casino in Henderson to play some slots. She has every reason to feel optimistic. After all, less than a year earlier, she hit a $1 million jackpot on a penny slot machine at Sunset Station.

This time around, after investing about 35 bucks over 10 minutes, JoAnn does it again. She wins yet *another* $1 million on a penny slot machine. Gambling experts instantly tout her as the "luckiest woman alive," and the national media is quick to grab hold of this feel-good story.

"My daughter looked over at the machine, and said, 'Mom, you did it again," JoAnn told Associated Press. "When

I realized it, I just put my head on her shoulder and cried."

Anthony Curtis, president of lasvegasadvisor.com, says JoAnn's odds of winning a second $1 million in less than a year is "in either the billions or trillions."

According to the article, Nevada gaming regulations allow her prize to be awarded in annual installments of $50,000 for 20 years. Instead, JoAnn accepts a lump sum payment of more than $400,000 after taxes and fees – just like she did after the first jackpot. Maybe, if she would have taken the annual payments, JoAnn's life might end up differently. Maybe a simple, steady flow of income like that over two decades would have kept her – and her son – a little more grounded. She would still be receiving that money today.

JoAnn reportedly uses the winnings from her first jackpot to "pay off her mortgage, remodel her house and take 10 family members on a cruise to Mexico. After this second jackpot, she starts planning a trip with her grandson.

"He immediately wanted to know where we were going," she says. "I'm thinking Hawaii."

When you combine this enormous luck with a hefty spousal support payment from her ex-husband, one of the founders of the once-popular Cherokee clothing line, it is hard to imagine how JoAnn could end up where she does. After once being celebrated as the world's luckiest gambler, in just a few years she will lose her only son, Pete, and maybe even her freedom. Then again, maybe her luck has not quite run out.

I am able to obtain court documents related to JoAnn's case. On July 3, 2018, JoAnn accepts a plea agreement in which all but one of the charges are dropped. On Sept. 26, 2018, she is sentenced to 5 years probation and ordered to pay $1,337,524.27 in restitution to the Colorado Casualty Insurance Company. Some reasoning for the much lighter sentence is offered in the court document.

"Argyris has pleaded guilty pursuant to a theory of being willfully blind to the actions of the prime mover of the mail fraud scheme, her now deceased son, Peter Argyris. While Argyris is nevertheless culpable for the scheme, having knowingly received its benefits and permitted its full execution, her criminal conduct appears to have been motivated to a certain degree by a misguided sense of maternal attachment. . . "

Pete Argyris dies on Sept. 27, 2017. The autopsy report lists cause of death as "acute combined drug toxicity," and the manner of death as "accidental."

Just when I think I have reached a conclusion to this case, I find something very interesting in the arson investigator's case file under the heading, "CONFIDENTIAL."

> "It was learned from Brandon's cell phone, which was located in a rental mini-van that was parked next door at a restaurant parking lot that on Sept. 19, 2010 at 03:31 hrs, there was an attempted outgoing phone call made to an unknown number. When Brandon's cell phone was used, he had been dead for 2 hours, 47 minutes."

> "This imperial data suggest that there was another person on the scene with Brandon, who either prematurely threw a flare or open flame into the gas-soaked structure that accidentally killed Brandon or threw a flare or open flame into the structure with the intent to kill Brandon . . . "

Were Brandon and Pete the only ones involved that night? Is Pete the one who made the outgoing call? Or, is there a third party out there somewhere feeling relieved he is not sitting in a prison cell right now.

CHAPTER 12 – TOM AND ZIMBA

It is Sunday morning on June 12, 1994 in Tehachapi, Calif., a beautiful mountain community southeast of Bakersfield. Tom and Amy Lang are teeing off at the Horse Thief Country Club, where they are interested in buying some property. It is the perfect way to end a perfect weekend getaway.

The No. 1 song on the pop charts is "I Swear," by the soulful, sweet-singing quartet known as All-4-One.

Speed, the action-thriller starring Keanu Reeves and Sandra Bullock, filmed right here in Southern California, is wrapping up a huge opening weekend, grossing $14.5 million. Few movies have ever been more flattering of the Los Angeles Police Department. Jack Travern, the young and handsome SWAT officer, risks his life to save a loaded transit bus from exploding into bits as it whizzes along an LA freeway. In less than a week, 95 million people will watch a real-life freeway "chase" that moves much slower, yet with so much more suspense.

After they complete their round of golf, the Lang's take a 4-hour drive to Orange County, where their 3-year-old daughter is staying with Amy's sister. Instead of spending the night, the couple decides to go ahead and drive home to Brentwood, a wealthy, trendy neighborhood in West Los

Angeles. Tom, a highly successful general contractor for Fujita Corporation, has some important work to do the next morning. His company is very involved with rebuilding Los Angeles after a major earthquake six months earlier.

By the time they reach their home at 975 South Bundy Drive late Sunday evening, everybody is understandably tired. Tom carries his sleeping daughter to bed before walking into the master bedroom. Amy throws their suitcase on the bed.

"How about you unpack the suitcase, and I will walk the dog?" Tom asks.

As he and his dog, Zimba, a very large Rhodesian ridgeback, walk out the front the door, Tom notices the digital clock in the living room change times. It is *exactly* 10 p.m. They exit the home and proceed north along the sidewalk on Bundy Drive. They are on the west side of the street. Tom and Zimba have taken this same stroll up Bundy Drive every single day with few exceptions for the past four years.

Zimba is a beautiful, well-trained dog that responds immediately to his master's commands. For this reason, even though it might rub some of his neighbors the wrong way, Tom is comfortable walking Zimba without a leash – especially this late at night.

In about two minutes, Tom and Zimba are within 75 feet of the intersection of Bundy Drive and Dorothy Street. At this moment, Tom hears a woman's voice. It is sometime between 10:02 and 10:03.

"It was very loud. I heard a commotion," Tom says. "It was a woman's loud voice. I don't know if she was singing or having sex. I have no idea. I just know it was loud."

Tom always turns left at this corner, but he likes to cross Dorothy first because the only sidewalk is on that side of the street. As Tom prepares to cross, he sees the headlights of three vehicles coming in his direction down Bundy Drive.

On most nights, Tom can determine immediately if a vehicle is signaling to turn west on Dorothy where he and his dog are about to cross. However, something is different on this evening.

"As I stood there, I couldn't see if the three cars coming down had their blinker on, which meant I couldn't go across the street with the dog because they might be turning right. Something was blocking my view."

Tom gives Zimba the command to "wait," then he takes a few steps out on Bundy to get a better look up the street. At this moment, he notices a "white Ford full-size truck vehicle" with its passenger door open parked next to the curb at 875 South Bundy Drive.

Yes . . . *that* 875 South Bundy Drive. In 12 more minutes, according to Marcia Clark's timeline, the brutal murder of Ron and Nicole is going to happen.

Tom estimates he has walked to this corner with Zimba more than 1,200 times over the previous four years. Nothing has ever blocked his view before, and he will later discover the reason why. There is a bus stop at this location, and parking is prohibited.

After the cars pass by safely without turning, Tom gives Zimba the command to "go." Zimba immediately darts across the street in the direction of a large palm tree, which is one of his favorite potty stops. However, the opened passenger door of that truck is directly behind the tree.

"I see the movement of a body at the door, and I know the dog is going to run to that tree and lift his leg. Don't want that."

Tom quickly gives the command of "Zimba . . . Hup!" followed by a hand signal to follow him west on Dorothy.

At that moment, a woman steps out from behind the passenger door and gives Tom a glare. The woman is about average height with blonde hair. She is wearing dark clothing. She looks down and notices Zimba, then shuts the passenger door. Tom does not know the woman's name, but he remembers seeing her before. She is the same woman who likes to drive fast in the alley behind his house.

By now, Tom is on the sidewalk on the north side of Dorothy. He gives one last look towards the truck and notices a second person — a White male — standing about 50 feet past the woman in the middle of the sidewalk on Bundy. He is about 5 feet, 11 inches and 175 pounds, also wearing dark clothing. The man appears to be angry. His knees are slightly bent with his fists clenched. Tom figures the man is upset because his dog is without a leash.

Tom continues west on Dorothy until he gets to Gretna Green Way. Like most nights, he plans to turn south on Gretna Green, and then around the block before returning home. First, he must cross Dorothy again in the opposite direction. He looks to his left to check for oncoming traffic and then notices that same "white Ford full-sized truck vehicle" turn in the alley behind 875 South Bundy.

"I didn't watch it long enough to see a side profile, to see if it was a pickup truck, a cargo van . . . a white Bronco. I didn't look. I just kept going."

Tom does not give his brief encounter at the now infamous northwest corner of Bundy Drive and Dorothy Street a second thought. He simply returns home and calls it a night, like he has done so many times before.

At 5:30 a.m., Tom's alarm goes off. As he gets ready for work, he has no idea about the chaos unfolding up the street. His car is parked in the rear of his property, so he takes the back alley south to Mayfield Avenue and turns right, then left on Gretna Green, then right on Wilshire Boulevard, then to his office at the Champagne Towers.

As soon as he walks into his office, Tom knows he is in for a rough day. Two high-ranking officials at Fujita Corporation have their yellow legal pads out, and they are unloading all of sorts of complicated engineering physics on Tom.

"I was supposed to be in charge, but I had no idea in the world what they were doing," Tom laughs.

When Tom returns home from work Monday evening, he still is not aware of . . . *the news.* This is 1994. Cell phones look more like walkie-talkies than smart phones. The Internet is still in its infancy. DirecTV is going to launch its multi-channel digital satellite service for the first time in three days from now. Bottom line: Many Americans are still relying on newspapers, television sets, and word of mouth.

Tom pours himself a stiff drink and sits down in the living room to watch television. He selects something easy for his fried brain. Even on a good day, he is not the type to sit and watch TV news.

"I was just mentally drained," Tom says. "Amy was trying to tell me something, but I just put my hand up. I was totally exhausted."

Meanwhile, NBC Nightly News is among many outlets who are all over the big story up the street.

> *"The body of 34-year-old Nicole Brown Simpson,*
> *ex-wife of OJ Simpson, was found after midnight*
> *on the sidewalk outside her west Los Angeles home,"*
> *says reporter Larry Carroll. "Next to it. . . the body*
> *of a 26-year-old unidentified man. Both had appar-*
> *ently been stabbed.*
>
> *"Simpson told police he was in Chicago at the time*
> *of the killings. He arrived at the home 12 hours*
> *after the bodies were discovered. Police escort-*
> *ed him to the rear of the building, and a short time*
> *later, Simpson was seen in handcuffs. After a confer-*
> *ence with Simpson's attorney, Howard Weitzman,*
> *Simpson was released from the cuffs and taken to*
> *police headquarters for questioning."*

The news report includes footage of a man and woman from the local coroner's office wheeling away a covered body underneath some caution tape and placing it in a van parked on Bundy. The caution tape is tied around a large palm tree.

Yes, *that* palm tree. Zimba's favorite palm tree.

On Tuesday morning, Tom does his normal get-ready routine and leaves for work again through the back alley. Still unaware of the double murders up the street, Tom is pleased to know he will have somewhat of a reprieve from the previous workday. His bosses are busy with other projects. He says good morning to his secretary, Marcy, then he walks into his office and sits down at his desk.

About 30 minutes later, Tom comes out of his office holding up a copy of the Los Angeles Times front page. Marcy can tell that something is wrong.

"Mr. Lang, I know you're White, but today you're *really* white," Marcy says.

Tom is visibly shaking.

"Marcy . . . I was there."

CHAPTER 13 – FINDING TOM

To avoid any confusion, you may notice there are two people involved with this case that share the same name, with the exception of one letter "e."

The first one is Tom Lange, one of the lead detectives assigned to the case. He is also the voice behind the man who tries to convince O.J. to surrender during the slow-speed chase on June 17, 1994.

> *Lange: Hey, it's going to be better tomorrow. Get rid of the gun. Toss it, please. Too many people love you, man. Don't give it all up. Don't hurt everybody. You're going to hurt everybody.*

> *Simpson: I'm just going to leave. I'm just going to go with Nicole. That's all I'm going to do. That's all I'm trying to do.*

The second is the lesser-known Tom Lang – without an "e." Even though he is unfamiliar to most, attorney F. Lee Bailey later describes Lang as possibly ". . . the only person who could have gotten a glimpse of the killer (or killers) that fateful evening."

Although most details of the murders and the subsequent investigation are yet to be revealed publicly, Tom Lang certainly appreciates the potential significance of what he saw just after 10 p.m. on June 12, 1994 at the corner of Bundy Drive and Dorothy Street.

Still shaken by what he just read on the LA Times front page, Tom shares his own story of that night with his boss, William Wells, vice president of Fujita North America. Wells, who is also an attorney, advises Tom to contact law enforcement immediately. Tom remembers his wife has a good friend who is an officer with the Santa Monica Police Department, so he makes a phone call. The officer tells Tom to put down his witness statement in writing and get it to the authorities.

Tom does one better. After he makes an 8-page handwritten statement, Tom sits down with Mr. Wells and records a witness statement on audio tape. Mr. Wells then calls a legal courier who delivers the tape and the written statement to the Los Angeles County District Attorney's Office before the close of business.

By now, it is already clear that O.J. Simpson is the prime suspect – if not the only suspect – in the murders of his wife and Ron Goldman. The Hall of Fame running back's potential involvement is the lead story on the evening news.

"Good evening . . . O.J. Simpson, one of America's best known sports and entertainment personalities, remains secluded in his Los Angeles home tonight as reports and rumors about his possible connection to his ex-wife's murder are getting wide play," says Tom Brokaw, news anchor for NBC News.

The news report provides the first details of evidence collected at both 875 Bundy Drive and O.J. Simpson's home at 360 North Rockingham Avenue. The evidence incudes blood-soaked gloves found at both properties, reddish-brown blood stains on Simpson's driveway and some white tennis shoes. There is also footage of a *"four-wheel drive Ford Bronco registered to Hertz Rent-a-Car, a company Simpson has pitched for years in television commercials,"* getting towed away as evidence.

The next day, on June 15, Simpson replaces his long-time attorney, Howard Weitzman, with a new lawyer, Robert Shapiro. It is one of the first steps in the creation of Simpson's "Dream Team" of defense lawyers, but the *real* All-Stars on this team have yet to be signed. In his first appearance in front of TV cameras, Shapiro appears to struggle through a slow and deliberate statement on OJ's behalf.

". . . At the time that this murder took place, O.J. was at home waiting to get into a limousine to take him to the airport," claims Shapiro in his first press statement. ". . . O.J. will do everything he can to cooperate with (police) to help solve this horrible murder."

As most of the media is digging into O.J. and Nicole's rocky marriage, including tales of domestic violence, some journalists are trying to learn more about the young waiter named Ronald Goldman. A headline from the LA Times on June 15 reads, "Murder Victim Called Free Spirit and Caring Friend."

> *". . . On the surface, it seemed that Ronald Lyle Goldman was living the exciting celebrity-centered life that draws good-looking young people to*

*Los Angeles from across the country to hover at the
fringes of Hollywood as waiters, tennis coaches and
fitness trainers," the article states.*

*"But friends portray Goldman, 25, as a nice guy
willing to go out of his way to help a friend rather than as a hanger-on entranced by the magic of
celebrity. And they speculate that it was Goldman's
innate helpfulness that drew him into his final
encounter with fame."*

One of Goldman's friends who is quoted in the article is a
young man named Pete Argyris.

On Thursday, June 16, Simpson is among several people attending his ex-wife's private funeral service in Los
Angeles. Another funeral for Ronald Goldman takes place
the same day in Agoura, Calif. Pete Argyris is one of the
pallbearers.

On Friday, June 17, Shapiro goes to an undisclosed home
in San Fernando Valley to inform O.J. that murder charges
have been filed. He is scheduled to surrender at 11 a.m.
When he does not show, LAPD announces that Simpson is
a fugitive. At 5 p.m., Simpson's friend, Robert Kardashian,
reads what many people believe is a suicide letter.

*"... Don't feel sorry for me. I've had a great life,
great friends. Please think of the real O.J. and not
this lost person. Thanks for making my life special. I
hope I helped yours. Peace and love. O.J."*

Less than hour later, Simpson makes a 911 call from a
cellphone in the Bronco. California High Patrol locates
Simpson on Interstate 5 in Orange County, not far from the

cemetery where Nicole was buried. The "chase," if that is what you want to call it, is on.

Meanwhile, Tom Lang is anxious to get home after what has obviously been a taxing week. Unfortunately, traffic in and around Brentwood is at a standstill. When Tom later learns that O.J., now in custody, is the reason for his delay getting home, he is slightly annoyed.

That frustration continues over the weekend as the tabloid media invades Tom's normally peaceful neighborhood. Reporters and wanna-be private eyes are knocking on doors looking for anybody who knows anything. One by one, Tom politely tells them to kick rocks. While other so-called witnesses are quick to sell their story for a few extra bucks, Tom and his wife prefer to have their privacy.

On Monday, June 20, a somber O.J. Simpson, with Shapiro by his side, appears in Los Angeles Municipal Court for his arraignment. Shapiro will later describe him as on medication and "very, very depressed . . . exceedingly emotional." O.J. clearly needs Shapiro's help answering questions from the court before finally entering a plea of "Not Guilty."

The arraignment is also much of the world's introduction to Deputy District Attorney Marcia Clark, the prosecutor assigned to the case. Even though Tom Lang's story, if she knew about it, could at least have offered her a reason to pause, Clark has already made up her mind eight days after the murders. She tells reporters outside the courthouse that she has no plans to charge anyone else for the killings.

"Mr. Simpson is charged alone . . . because he is the sole murderer," Clark says.

That same night, at 8:30 p.m., Tom gets a knock on his door at 975 South Bundy Drive – exactly one block down from the crime scene. Expecting to give another reporter another quick rejection, this person at the door is wearing a badge. The man introduces himself as Detective Dennis Payne from the Los Angeles Police Department's Robbery-Homicide Division.

During a short interview in the living room, Tom wonders if Detective Payne really has his full attention, or if he is just going through the motions. He wonders why Payne has not invited him up the street to retrace his steps. An LA Times article dated July 28, 1994 identifies Payne as LAPD's "designated clue chaser" for this high-profile case. The department is receiving hundreds of tips every day, and if police do not at least appear to follow up, the defense team will be quick to point that out to a jury down the road.

"There's people that are giving us theories, there's psychics, that kind of thing," Payne tells the Times. "And then there's people who have information. We're checking it all out."

After saying goodbye to Tom, Detective Payne sits down and types up his police report, which for some reason has glaring differences to the written statement Tom submitted just six days earlier.

". . . As he reached the corner of the intersection, he observed a female white, with shoulder length blond hair, and wearing some type of *light colored flowing dress or gown* standing on the parkway next to the passenger door of the vehicle, facing a tall male, NFD (No Further Description). They appeared to be embracing," Payne writes.

Light colored flowing dress or gown? Embracing? Strange. Tom's statement, handwritten in all caps, offers a largely different account:

". . . SHE LOOKED AT ME THEN AT THE DOG THEN BACK TOWARD BUNDY AT THE TRUCK PARKED THERE

(SHE WAS MED. HT. – BLOND – IN DARK CLOTHING). I COULD NOT SEE WHO WAS STANDING ON THE PASSENGER SIDE OF THE TRUCK BECAUSE THE DOOR WAS HALF OPEN AND THE TREE WAS BLOCKING MY VIEW. . . "

Twenty-seven years later, in his book titled, "The Truth About the O.J. Simpson Trial," attorney F. Lee Bailey will allege that Payne's "short" police report was falsified.

The police report also describes the vehicle Tom observed parked facing south on the west side of Bundy Drive as a "white Ford truck, NFD. . . "

"The truck was partially concealed by a parkway palm tree, but Mr. Lang, who owns several Ford vehicles, recognized the logo on the front of the vehicle and the shape of the vehicle as that of a full size passenger vehicle," Payne writes. "He did not notice whether the engine was running or if any vehicle lights were illuminated."

Payne's report also refers to that "third person," which is more consistent with Tom's story.

". . . a male White or Hispanic standing on the sidewalk approximately 50 feet north of the vehicle and Mr. Lang. The man was wearing a short sleeve shirt and long pants and had assumed an angry stance, slightly bent at the waist and with both fists clenched," Payne writes. "Mr. Lang believed the man was possibly angry at him for walking his dog on the sidewalk without a leash. The man did not make any move toward him and Mr. Lang walked out of view, west on Dorothy Street."

Tom Lang does not consider himself a potential witness for the defense. Like so many of Nicole's neighbors, he believes that O.J. is the likely murderer. However, he also stands firm that "what I saw is 100 percent what I saw." He is not able to confirm either way if that Ford vehicle parked on Bundy was a pick-up truck or a Bronco. He just does not get a good enough look at it.

As the preliminary hearings get underway June 30, Tom fully expects to receive a call from Marcia Clark's office. That call never happens. Four other neighbors, along with several other witnesses, will testify during the preliminary hearings, but Tom Lang is not one of them.

At this time, the so-called Dream Team still does not exist and Bailey is only helping Shapiro as a consultant. As such, Bailey recommends that Shapiro hire two private investigators. One of them is John McNally of New York. The other is Patrick McKenna of Florida. Patrick McKenna . . . why does this name ring a bell?

After a quick Google search, I have my answer. I realize my wife and I just watched McKenna appear in documentary series on Peacock about another high-profile case that captured America's attention in 2008. Long after working for Shapiro & Co. on the O.J. case, McKenna became the lead investigator in the defense of Casey Anthony, charged and later acquitted of murdering her two-year-old daughter, Caylee.

Like Simpson, Casey Anthony, once touted as "The Most Hated Mom in America," still loses heavily in the court of public opinion to this day. McKenna, however, is by far Casey's strongest supporter. After the trial is over, McKenna allows Casey to move into his family's home in West Palm Beach and helps her get back on her feet.

On Friday, Feb. 10, 2023, McKenna receives an unexpected phone call from a school principal in Arizona. I tell him that I'm writing a book that is somewhat related to the O.J. case, but I am specifically interested in a man named

Tom Lang. Much to my delight, McKenna agrees to a phone interview with me the following morning.

When I saw McKenna in the Casey Anthony documentary, I remember having a certain level of admiration for the man. He came across as a real straight shooter who believed strongly in his friend's innocence. My opinion does not change during my two-hour interview about Tom Lang. He talks very candidly about the importance of Tom Lang's story and his unsuccessful efforts to persuade The Dream Team to put him on the stand. He drops a few F-bombs here and there, which, honestly, I like. McKenna is also convinced – now more than ever – that O.J. is innocent.

"I know it could have not been OJ," McKenna tells me. "He just didn't have time to do everything they think he did."

Ten days after my phone interview, McKenna sends me an email with several attachments, including a copy of Tom's handwritten notes, the police report, McKenna's internal memo to the defense team and more. Even a photo of Tom's dog. I have struck gold.

It is impossible to describe my excitement as I read all these documents related to Tom Lang. The other Tom Lang. The Tom Lang without an "e" at the end. However, I begin to realize I need to take it a step further. When I ask McKenna if Tom Lang is still around, he tells me he thinks he is living in Central California somewhere.

"Maybe over by Bakersfield or somewhere close to that."

It is weird to imagine this Tom Lang guy sitting in his home in California's heartland somewhere knowing what he knows. Does he want to tell his story? I suppose, if he did, he would have done it by now. I know this: If I am truly going to give Tom Lang's story the full attention it deserves, it should not come from an investigator in Florida. I need to find Tom Lang.

By now, I am fairly proficient at using my paid web site service for finding people. However, when I enter "Thomas Lang" and "California," hundreds of names pop up. They are listed by name and age, and I do not know how old Mr. Lang is . . . or do I?

I know I have a copy of the police report, so maybe there is a "DOB" next to Mr. Lang's name somewhere. There is, but it has been redacted. Bummer. I scroll through the other documents to McKenna's memo. Sure enough, below his name at the top of the page is his exact date of birth. Tom will turn 71 later this year.

Now all I have to do is look for a 70-year-old named Thomas Lang living in California. Not 68 or 73. My Tom Lang is 70. I scroll down near the bottom of the page, and I find one. What are the chances this is my guy? I click "Open Report." At the top of the web page is a phone number and current address for a Thomas Lang living in Tehachapi. I know Tehachapi. It is a beautiful mountain community east of Bakersfield. My late Aunt Linda used to live there.

I scroll down further to the portion that says "Prior Addresses." Sure enough. Clear as day. There it is.

975 South Bundy Drive.

This *has* to be him.

I will not feel right if I do not at least try to get the first-ever media interview with a man who might have seen the actual killer or killers – whether it was O.J. Simpson or anybody else for that matter. I call the phone number at the top. Straight to voicemail, of course.

I leave a message, wait a few days, and leave another. After five unreturned messages, it is time to try something else. I enter a Google search of "Tom Lang Tehachapi." I do not see anything about Tom, but I do get a couple of hits on an Amy Lang, who just happens to be a science teacher at Tehachapi Middle School. Maybe this is my foot in the door.

I send Mrs. Lang an email.

> "... If you could please pass along this request to Tom, I would be most grateful. If you have already received messages from me, I'm sorry to bug. I just think it's very important to include his story in my book. On a side note, thanks for everything you do as a teacher. You are super heroes."

Three days later, I receive a phone call from a number I do not recognize.

"Hello?"

"Hello, is this Mr. Wedemeyer?"

"Yes, it is."

"This is Tom Lang."

CHAPTER 14 – TOM'S DAY IN COURT

At the conclusion of the preliminary hearings on July 8, 1994 Judge Kathleen Kennedy-Powell rules that O.J. will stand trial for the murders of Nicole and Ron. He is taken into custody without bail. On July 22, Simpson appears before Judge Lance Ito at Los Angeles County Superior Court to enter his plea, and he is not the same sad puppy who appeared at the start of the preliminary hearings.

"Absolutely 100 percent not guilty," O.J. declares.

Meanwhile, Tom Lang still has not heard anything from Marcia Clark's office. He wonders if Detective Payne really took him seriously, and if this double murder case is simply going to move along without him.

However, those feelings change on Aug. 8, 1994, when Tom gets another knock on the door. The man introduces himself as Patrick McKenna, a private investigator working for Robert Shapiro. Tom notices that Mr. McKenna is wearing a tie and conducting himself in a very professional manner compared to the other yahoos who have knocked on the door over the previous several weeks.

To prove that he is who he says he is, McKenna hands Tom a letter from Shapiro himself.

"Dear Mr. Lang:

*This letter will confirm that Patrick J. McKenna
and John E. McNally are employed by my law firm
as investigators in the case of People vs. Orenthal
James Simpson.*

*Your willingness to cooperate as a witness in our
investigation is very much appreciated.*

*If you have any questions, please don't hesitate to
contact me.*

Thank you again for your assistance.

Sincerely,

Robert L. Shapiro.

Tom invites McKenna inside, and after some introductions,
the interview begins. Unlike Detective Payne, McKenna appears to Tom as very engaged, asking follow-up questions
and taking detailed notes.

"I would have put down everything he said," McKenna
tells me almost 30 years later. "I don't care if it's good, bad
or ugly. I'll take it as long as it's the truth. It doesn't matter to
me. I just want to know what you know."

What Tom does *not* know is that McKenna has already
read Detective Payne's report. When Tom refers to seeing a blonde woman in dark clothing that night in front of
Nicole's condo, McKenna pauses. He pulls out the police
report and shows Tom what Detective Payne typed up, ". . .
he observed a female, with shoulder length blonde hair, and
wearing some type of light colored flowing dress or gown."

Tom is livid.

"That ain't what the fuck I said," he tells McKenna. "I never said anything about a white flowing gown."

Also unlike Detective Payne, McKenna is anxious to retrace Tom's steps from that night – from start to finish. They keep track of the time and distance before stopping at the exact spot Tom stood that fateful evening. Three minutes have gone by since leaving the house.

"He said that a Ford F350 model truck was parked at the bus stop with the front passenger door partially open, the bus sign blocked it from being open completely," McKenna writes in his memo to the defense team 11 days later.

"Lang told us he has owned 11 Ford vehicles, and he was positive that the white Ford truck was a F350 model."

To be fair, that is not what Tom tells me 29 years later, and that is not what he describes in his written statement to authorities two days after the murders.

". . . MY VIEW WAS BLOCKED BY A WHITE FORD TRUCK TYPE (vehicle)."

McKenna and Tom touch base a few times over the next several months, but there is no contact from defense lawyers. He also still has not heard a word from Marcia Clark and her crew. The criminal trial begins on Jan. 24, 1995.

Marcia Clark and Deputy District Attorney Christopher Darden both contribute to the prosecution's opening statement. In essence, Darden starts his remarks by breaking down *why* the murders happened.

". . . He killed Nicole—not because he hated her. He didn't hate Nicole. He didn't kill her because he didn't love her anymore. He killed for a reason almost as old as mankind itself," Darden says. "He killed her out of jealousy. He killed her because he couldn't have her. And if he couldn't have her, he didn't want anybody else to have her. He killed her to control her."

Clark, on the other hand, gives the jury a preview of the evidence explaining *how* it happened, including her first public declaration on the alleged time of the murders.

". . . And so, the evidence will prove that Kato (Brian Kaelin) last saw the defendant on the night of June the 12th at 9:35 at the latest. He did not see the defendant again until after 11:00," Clark says. "In between those two times, at 10:15, a dog is heard barking that the evidence will show was Nicole's dog, which fixes the time at which the murder occurred."

By this time, Johnnie Cochran, regarded by some as one of the top trial lawyers in the country, has replaced Shapiro as the undisputed leader of The Dream Team. He delivers his opening remarks for the defense the following morning.

One hour and 25 minutes into his opening statement, Cochran attempts to address some of Clark's assertions about the "timeline and evidence trails." This is the first moment when Tom Lang – without the "e," and without much fanfare, becomes a part of the trial's official record:

". . . There's a Mr. Tom Lang, that she knows about, and she didn't tell you about, who on this particular night, on June 12, 1994, was walking his dog, on a street called Dorothy Street, right down the way from Nicole Brown Simpson's condo at 875. . . . That from his vantage point. . . just a short distance on the corner. . . He looked up and saw a lady that he believes was Ms. Nicole Brown Simpson embracing someone at a vehicle at the curb. . . and behind Ms. Simpson, he saw a man that he described as a Hispanic or Caucasian, standing with his hands clenched. . . standing there looking as though he was angry. And he didn't know why this man was looking like this. This is about 10 o'clock on June 12th. Mr. Lang didn't know whether he was angry because his dog was loose or what."

Embracing someone?

In Tom's handwritten statement from June 14, when his memory is still fresh, he says nothing about an embrace.

"I COULD NOT SEE WHO WAS STANDING ON THE PASSENGER SIDE OF THE TRUCK BECAUSE THE DOOR WAS HALF OPEN AND THE TREE WAS BLOCKING MY VIEW."

Cochran and his team obviously have pulled this from Detective Payne's report, which states, ". . . and wearing some type of light colored flowing dress or gown standing on the parkway next to the passenger door of the vehicle, facing a tall male, NFD. They appeared to be embracing."

How do two statements from the same person — one in his own writing, and one in an official police report – made just six days part, have such glaring and critical contradictions? Defense attorney F. Lee Bailey, for some reason, offers even a third take of the encounter in his book, "The Truth About the O.J. Simpson Trial."

"Standing in the street next to the truck was a blonde woman dressed in dark clothing whom Lang thought was arguing with a passenger in the truck," Bailey writes.

So which is it? Were they embracing or arguing or none of the above? I am going to stick with Tom's own written statement. He could not *see* who was standing on the passenger side, so he certainly would not know if they were embracing or arguing.

A front-page article on the LA Times the following morning highlights much of Cochran's opening statement, but makes no mention of Tom Lang.

On July 11, during Christopher Darden's cross-examination of a witness named Francesca Harman, Tom Lang's name comes up again – seemingly out of nowhere. Harman has just testified that she left a party before arriving at the corner of Dorothy Street and Bundy Drive at exactly 10:20 p.m. As she turns north on Bundy directly in front of Nicole's condo, she does not see or hear any commotion – no barking dogs, no arguing, etc.

DARDEN: "Do you know a man named Tom Lang?"

Harman, who has already identified herself as a convention services manager for a local hotel, has to think about this question for a moment.

HARMAN: "I. . . . I do."

DARDEN: "Does Tom Lang work for the same company you work for?"

HARMAN: "He doesn't work for the same company. He is just located in the same building."

Darden has nothing further. However, at least now it is clear that the prosecution knows about Tom Lang and what he might testify. While his last three questions to Harman might seem a little off topic to the millions watching from home, F. Lee Bailey is paying close attention.

The following morning, Judge Ito is just about to call in jurors to hear more witness testimony when Bailey suddenly stands up and asks to speak.

BAILEY: "Yesterday you heard a reference to a witness Lang, and you heard a reference to a white truck during the cross examination of Francesca Harman by Mr. Darden. I discovered yesterday for the first time since we have been working on Mr. Lang that a tape recording of his observations that night was made almost immediately after the events and turned over to the prosecution many months ago together with a sketch of what he saw.

"And he says that at 10 o'clock at night he saw a large white truck, somebody in the truck, a blonde woman he now recognizes as Nicole Brown Simpson, discoursing with the person in the truck, and someone standing near the entrance to her gate in a menacing posture of Caucasian or Asian descent.

"Now I think it's an absolute outrage that this clearly exculpatory evidence putting her in the company of someone else who could possibly have figured into these murders has not turned been turned over to the defense. I ask that you order that it be turned over forthwith, and we find out why it wasn't."

DARDEN: What are we talking about Heidstra or Lang?

BOTH BAILEY AND ITO: "Lang."

Even though he just asked Francesca Harman about Tom Lang the day before, Darden, casually shrugging his shoulders with his hands in his front pockets, is quick to pass the buck.

DARDEN: "That's Miss Clark's witness, your honor. I haven't heard a tape of Mr. Lang."

"Do you know anything about a sketch?" the judge asks.

"No."

Ito informs Bailey that he intends to get the scoop on this Tom Lang matter during a break when Marcia Clark returns. Then things get a little testy as they do often during this trial.

BAILEY: "I'm sure Mr. Darden will convey to her my concerns."

DARDEN: (mumbling) "You can convey them yourself."

ITO: "Excuse me, Mr. Darden, direct your comments to the court . . . not the counsel."

Later that afternoon, it is Marcia Clark's turn to address the court about Tom Lang, the tape, and the sketch.

Clark tells the court that she does not have a taped statement, because when Detective Payne received a copy from Tom Lang, "it had a seminar on one side, and it was blank on the other." She adds that when the detective asked for another copy, Tom told him "he lost it and couldn't find it and never did give him one."

"I understand now that the tape in fact does exist, that it's in the possession of Mr. Lang's lawyer who is currently transcribing it," Clark says. "Mr. Bailey will pick it up this afternoon and we will pick up a copy from him."

Then Marcia Clark offers a hint that maybe Tom Lang was very close to telling the jurors his story that day.

"I thought that Mr. Lang was going to be testifying this afternoon having received no notice to the contrary until two minutes ago. . . "

Bailey seems comfortable with Marcia Clark's explanation of the tape. However, he is still "pressing" for the sketch that he says was given to a police officer.

Responded Clark, "I don't have an understanding that any police officer received any sketch."

Bailey insists that someone connected with the prosecution received both a sketch as well as Tom Lang's written statement.

When the issue is brought up again later that day, another defense attorney, Carl Douglas, gets into the fight. He tells the court that Tom Lang was previously on the prosecution witness list back in September, but his name was removed from an updated list from Jan. 5. He argues that the so-called sketch should have been turned over when it was first received.

Gary Hodgman, a prosecuting attorney, confirms that Tom Lang was on the prosecution witness list at one point, but not anymore.

"We did not intend to call Mr. Lang as a witness for reasons personal to ourselves, and as evidenced by our case in chief, he was not presented," Hodgman said.

Responded Douglas, "The test is not whether in actuality they are going to call him . . . We have been given thousands of pages of documents of interviews from witnesses who they haven't called, so that is not the test."

Judge Ito rules in favor of the defense, ordering the sketch to be disclosed forthwith.

When I interview Tom Lang in early 2023, even he has no idea he was the subject of this small legal entanglement that takes up a few hours of a grueling nine-month criminal trial. The national media does not give it any attention, so if you happened to stumble into the kitchen for a snack, you might have missed it.

Also, Tom tells me that he is unaware of any sketch. When I hear the word sketch in relation to a homicide, the first thing that comes to my mind is a suspect drawing. Maybe he draws a likeness of the "menacing" mystery man standing on the sidewalk. What I do have in my possession, sent to me in an email from Patrick McKenna, is a handwritten map on a small piece of blue paper. It resembles something a person might draw for a friend to give them directions. It shows the corner, and where the condo and the truck are located. That is it. It would have taken just a few minutes to produce. Tom tells me he might have drawn up something like that for the police officer, but he does not remember.

So how close does Tom Lang ever really get to the witness stand? Well, how about a few feet.

It is unclear as to the exact date, but at some point during the trial, Tom's pager goes off. It is from Robert Shapiro. Tom calls the number at 8 a.m. Instead of Mr. Shapiro on the other line, it is his wife of 25 years, Linell Shapiro, on the other end.

"Hi, this is Tom Lang."

"Oh, the detective?"

"No, the witness."

"Oh, hold on just a moment."

Tom can hear the sound of Linell's feet scampering into a bathroom. It is clear that Mr. Shapiro is in the shower. Linell gets back on the phone.

"Bob said to be at the court at 10 o'clock," Linell tells Tom.

A trusted co-worker agrees to drive Tom to the court-house, which, from the outside, looks more like a madhouse of news crews and curious onlookers. As Tom gets dropped off, he gives his driver a cell phone.

"Do not stop and pull over," Tom tells his co-worker. "Just keep circling around the courthouse and I will call you when I'm ready."

Tom steps out of the vehicle and immediately walks through a crowd of people to the largest police officer he can find. He pulls out a subpoena he received a few days earlier and gives it to the officer, who gives it a quick read.

"Ok, put that away," the officer says. "And follow me."

The officer escorts Tom into the courthouse to a nearby elevator. He waits briefly until he hears someone say, "Send him up."

When the elevator doors open, Tom immediately sees the entrance to Judge Ito's courtroom. A large female deputy sheriff instructs Tom to sit at a bench in the hallway.

He is there for just a moment when he gets a page from his co-worker outside.

"Hello? You stopped? No, no, no. Keep driving. I will call you."

A few minutes later, the deputy walks Tom over to the defense table, where he sits down in Shapiro's chair. Mr. Shapiro is not around, and Tom can't help but take a peek at some of the notes on the table in front of him.

"I guess I wanted to see if there was anything that says he is guilty," Tom says.

Marcia Clark is standing up front talking to a witness. It is none other than Detective Tom Lange – with an "e." What are the chances? I seem to ask this question a lot during this journey.

"Both Marcia and the detective we're looking at me like, 'Who's that?'" Tom says. "Neither one of them had ever met me."

At this moment, Johnny Cochran slides into the chair next to Tom and introduces himself.

"You've never heard anybody talk as fast as Johnny Cochran," Tom tells me.

Then, Cochran slows down just enough to ask Tom one very important question.

"By the way, did you see if it was a Bronco?"

Before Tom can answer, Marcia Clark, who was obviously eavesdropping, walks over to the table.

"Her ears pointed up like a Doberman Pincher," Tom says. "She slid into the table next to me so close that her face was almost touching mine."

At that point, Johnny Cochran shuts it down.

"Well, Mr. Lang, it really doesn't matter right now. I appreciate you coming," Cochran says. "Just stay home, and we'll let you know when you got to come back."

Tom follows Cochran's instructions. On the way home, he is uncertain why is his testimony is over before it starts.

"That was my day in court."

One can look to many reasons why the defense never calls Tom Lang to testify. Would the jury be swayed into thinking Tom actually saw O.J.'s Bronco? In his book, F. Lee Bailey offers another reason.

"Unfortunately, Lang was one of the important defense witnesses who was prevented from testifying because of the ticking clock," Bailey writes. "We had a dwindling jury pool, which became an increasing dark cloud that hovered over this trial from the start. . . "

Looking back, Tom has mixed feelings about never taking the stand. He firmly believes he saw something important on the evening of June 12, 1994, but he also is fully aware of the unwanted attention that comes with simply being associated to this case.

"I also had a young baby and a wife, and I was getting threats," Tom says. "In my opinion, this was the start of the world going down the toilet bowl, and I didn't want to have anything to do with it."

On Sept. 27, 1995, just 19 days after the murder of Michael Nigg in Hollywood, Darden continues with his closing argument that started the previous day. He calls out the defense, particularly Cochran, for promising to put some witnesses on the stand during his opening statement . . . and then not delivering.

"Apparently this sequestration thing is a real drag, right, and I would like to end this experience, and I can understand that, but he promised to present you with testimony of some witnesses who, had they testified, could have

– could have perhaps raised a reasonable doubt in this case. So where are all those people? Who are those people?"

Darden specifically asks about Rosa Lopez, a housemaid for O.J.'s neighbor who claims she saw the Bronco parked in front of his Rockingham estate just after 10 p.m. Her testimony is tape-recorded because she says she needs to return to her home country of El Salvador. The prosecution catches Lopez in several contradictions. She is not a strong witness for the defense, and the jury never sees the tape.

"Well, where is she? Where was she?" Darden asks the jury. "You would have liked to have heard that testimony, wouldn't you? He didn't call her."

Darden then asks about Mary Anne Gerchas, who claims she saw four men, some wearing knit caps, running from the crime scene at 10:45 p.m. on the night of the murders. Gerchas is arrested in June, 1995 and later pleads guilty to felony theft after failing to pay a hotel bill of more than $23,000, stealing jewelry and writing a bad check. The defense does not dare put her on the stand with that kind of shoddy credibility, and Darden takes full advantage.

"Did they call Mary Anne Gerchas? What happened to her? Where is that testimony? You would want to hear that, wouldn't you?"

Next on Darden's hit list is Tom Lang, a successful and respected general contractor, husband and father, helping to rebuild a broken city after a major earthquake. He is a man who believes O.J. is probably guilty, who never expected to be a witness for the defense, who the prosecution never bothered to interview, who never sold his story to a tabloid, and who has avoided the spotlight for nearly three decades. Now, Darden, for some reason, is lumping him in with the likes a Rosa Lopez and Mary Anne Gerchas.

". . . And right after they talked about Gerchas they talked about a man named Tom Lang who was supposedly down the street who also saw somebody," Darden tells the jury.

At this very moment, Tom Lang – without the "e" — is parked at a 7-11 convenience store in Los Angeles drinking his coffee and listening to Darden on his car stereo.

"They told you that Tom Lang saw Nicole Brown standing on the street at Bundy embracing – embracing someone, and that Tom Lang, as he stood there on the street, also saw a man standing a distance behind them, a man who appeared to be angry, a man standing there with his hands clenched looking at Nicole and this other person, the person she was embracing," Darden says. "It is right there in the transcript at page 12,225. Where is that person?"

Tom shakes his head.

"I'm right here . . . asshole."

CHAPTER 15 – THE 50-50 GUY

After the criminal trial is over, Tom Lang moves on with his life. His name does not come up during the 1996 civil trial that ends in a $33.5 million judgement for the families of Nicole and Ron, and he could not care less. Tom is more than content on the other side of O.J.'s moon where he will not be bothered.

Even though discussion and debate on this case never subsides, Tom has no interest. To this day, he has not read a single article about the murders. One day, his father called from the St. Louis airport to tell him his name was on the front page of the National Enquirer. Tom still has a copy of the tabloid somewhere, but he has never looked to see what is inside.

"I have never read one word about the case," Tom says. "I don't want to."

When asked why, Tom makes it clear he does not like wasting time and energy on O.J. Simpson.

"Obviously, I'm not happy about what happened in my neighborhood," says Tom, who still resides in Brentwood to this day.

Then, of course, there is the matter of the Trojan horse.

Prior to the 1984 Summer Olympics in Los Angeles, Tom

accepts a job remodeling a sports bar on the campus of USC. The owners hope to transform the sports bar into the No. 1 gathering spot during the Games.

However, when Tom, a UCLA graduate, walks into the sports bar for the first time, it is filled with what appears to be valuable USC sports memorabilia – pictures, jerseys, trophies, even a football signed by "The Juice" himself. Tom makes a call to USC, who immediately send people over to grab everything in the sports bar that is cardinal and gold.

However, when Tom returns the following day to begin work, one USC item still remains — a 4-by-4-foot picture of a Trojan horse set in stained glass above the bar. Tom needs to put a wide-screen television in that spot, so he carefully takes the picture down off the wall. The picture barely fits in his new GMC Blazer. He takes it back to his workshop, where it remains for several years until one of his construction buddies makes an inquiry.

"Hey Lang, you still got that horse?"

"Yeah, why?

"I'm going to be working on O.J.'s house, and we're doing a bar. How much do you want for it?

"Four grand."

"O.K."

The next time Tom Lang hears about O.J. Simpson, he is stopped at the intersection of 26th and Wilshire, where police have blocked off his normal route home to Bundy Drive. He pulls into a nearby restaurant/bar where several patrons are watching "the chase" unfold. You know the rest of the story, and the Trojan horse stays with Tom.

Several years later, after the O.J. trial is long over and Simpson is a free man – for now — a friend and attorney named Marla Anne Brown, a USC booster at the time, contacts Tom.

"You still got that horse?" Marla asks.

When Tom says yes, Marla suggests he sells the picture to O.J. himself, then O.J. can donate the picture back to USC. Before those arrangements are made, however, USC's Board of Regents bans Simpson from the campus. Again, the Trojan horse stays with Tom.

"Yeah, this Bruin still has that frickin' horse," Tom tells me.

In 2001, F. Lee Bailey, the man who defended the likes of Sam Sheppard, the Boston Strangler and Patty Hearst, loses his law license in Florida for mishandling shares of stock by a former client and convicted drug smuggler. Ten years later, he posts a 46-page position paper on his consulting company's web site, arguing that O.J. Simpson is innocent of the murders of Nicole and Ron. A few media outlets take notice of the paper, and Tom Lang's name comes up again. In fact, a headline on the ABA Journal's web site reads:

"F. Lee Bailey: Dog Walker Would Have Shown O.J. Simpson Wasn't a Murderer."

The article gives Bailey's description of Tom Lang's story, which again is not 100 percent aligned with Tom's own handwritten statement two days after the murders.

> *"Lang reports seeing a blonde woman arguing with a man near a white pickup – a Ford F350, not the Bronco owned by Simpson – on the night of the murder. Another man nearby had a 'menacing' posture, and he stood in a partially crouched position."*

"Lang could have answered the question, "If Simpson didn't do it, who did?""

I am anxious to read the entire position paper myself. Every web article I can find in 2023 includes a link to the position paper, but none of them is still functional. When I interview Tom Lang, he is unaware the position paper ever existed.

The article also reports that Bailey hopes the position paper will lead to a book someday. His wishes come true shortly before his death 10 years later with "The Truth About the O.J. Simpson Trial: By the Architect of the Defense."

Tom Lang's name first appears in the book on Page 37.

"Lang is a witness who never testified at the trial, but who may have been the only person who could have gotten a glimpse of the killer (or killers) that fateful evening. More important, this is the first time his name and witness account has ever been shared with the public."

Tom has never seen Bailey's book. When I read that paragraph to Tom over the phone, he is not bothered. Make no mistake. Tom Lang believes Simpson is guilty, and that belief has less to do with what he saw on June 12, 1994. It has everything to do with what Simpson allegedly said during a private meeting with attorneys that just happened to include one of Tom's colleagues. Tom will not reveal his identity.

After the private meeting, the colleague contacted Tom to say that his name came up during the conversation. As the group is discussing Tom's account of that night, Simpson allegedly makes a slip of the tongue. According to Tom, Simpson tells the group he does not remember seeing anybody out there.

"And he's right. I left before anything else happened," Tom tells me. "And Johnny Cochran had to remind him, that the only way he would know that, is if he was also there. In other words, shut up O.J., and don't ever say that again."

"And no one outside a couple of people in my life, and now you, have ever heard that."

Of course, Bailey's take on Tom Lang begs an obvious question. If Tom is such a "compelling witness," why didn't The Dream Team have him testify? Bailey attempts to address this issue towards the end of his book.

> "... Johnnie was hesitant to put him on the stand for reasons that he and I hotly debated in a closed-door meeting in June. It was, in the course of this long and demanding trial, the only time in which we disagreed in what could be considered a meaningful way."

Bailey says Cochran's concerns about Tom Lang was two-fold. First, is the police report, which describes a blonde woman in a "long, white dress." Nicole was wearing black at the time of her death.

> "However, this was an error on the part of the police record and not what Lang had told the reporting officer," Bailey writes. "Johnnie felt the faulty police record would be difficult to dispel and open a hole for the prosecution."

The second issue for Cochran, says Bailey, was the white truck. From the grill area, a Ford F350 and a Ford Bronco look very similar. (Again, Lang does not identify a specific model in his handwritten statement two days after the murders.)

". . . Johnnie thought it was another potential crack that the prosecutors could exploit to their advantage . . . After a brief, and somewhat passionate back and forth, Johnnie won out. . . "

Today, Tom still works in the construction industry in Los Angeles, specializing in elevators. He also owns property in Tehachapi – the same place he and his wife Amy went house hunting at during the weekend of June 12, 1994. He stays there on most weekends.

Tom even makes the local news in Tehachapi in 2013, when he sells his last 50-50 raffle ticket at a Tehachapi High School football game. Over a 12-year period that included 72 games, Tom raised nearly $15,000 for THS sports programs.

According to an article in the Tehachapi News, Tom was known for his creative sales pitches that encouraged family members and fans to open up their wallets.

"He would do the popular $20 pull, where he would reel out a roll of tickets as far as his arm could stretch, 7 tickets for $5, whatever he could do to get you to buy," wife Amy Lang tells the reporter. "He had fun with it and he even had regulars. They always knew my husband as the 50-50 guy."

Added City Councilman and Warriors PA announcer Ed Grimes, "Having Tom do this season-after-season has been a blessing. He has a gift. He truly cares about the kids, and his motivation and interaction with the fans all these years has really made the game fun. We'll miss that."

"I had a good run, but it's time for someone else to step in and take it over," says Lang in the article. "I had a lot of fun though, it's been great coming to the games all these years and making money for the program."

As a school principal and PA announcer for my home-town Parker High Broncs, this testimony about Tom Lang, above all others, means the most to me. Tom Lang is a good man. I believe what he has to say about June 12, 1994, and I wish somebody gave the jury an opportunity to hear his story.

I really struggle to understand why Marcia Clark's team never reaches out to Tom Lang to hear what he has to say. One short, simple conversation between Marcia and Tom could have been the difference.

CHAPTER 16 – THE OTHER DOG WALKER

If you are surprised like me about what happens to Tom Lang during the People vs. O.J. Simpson, you should consider the roller coaster ride of Robert Heidstra, the better-known dog walker from that night. Unlike Tom, Heidstra, a local car detailer, testifies in both the criminal and civil trials, and his story is the same in both.

Heidstra lives in an apartment complex on Dorothy Street east of Bundy Drive at the time of the murders. He walks his two small sheep dogs around the block three times a day – morning, afternoon and night. His evening stroll typically starts at 10 p.m., but on this night, he watches the news for a bit before taking off late at about 10:15.

Remember, 10:15 is the time when Marcia Clark says the murders take place.

Heidstra exits the complex and proceeds east on Dorothy – away from Bundy – then north on Westgate Avenue, then west on Gorham Avenue. At about 10:35 p.m., he nears the point at which Gorham begins to curve and merge with Bundy going south.

"Then I stopped because I heard all of a sudden from nowhere an Akita barking like crazy hell broke loose,"

Heidstra tells Johnny Cochran during the criminal trial. He later describes the dog's sounds as "hysterically panicking."

Heidstra normally continues down Bundy — along the sidewalk across the street from Nicole's condo each time — to Dorothy before turning left to go home. However, to avoid a confrontation with his own dogs, Heidstra says he turns around and takes a detour down the alley behind the houses on Bundy. He pauses a few times to listen to the dog, and he senses something is not right. He is somewhere across the street from Nicole's condo when he stops again to listen to the Akita from the alley. A small black dog in the alley also starts barking. Heidstra's dogs stay quiet, but remain alert.

At this moment, at about 10:40, Heidstra says he hears two voices.

Cochran: Alright. What did you hear these two voices say?

Heidstra: Well, the first one I heard was a clear male young adult voice that said, "Hey, hey, hey."

Heidstra adds that he then hears another voice "fast-talking" back to the person who says "Hey, hey, hey."

Cochran: Did you hear what the other voice said?

Heidstra: Could never hear. The dogs were barking so loud I couldn't hear nothing.

At about 10:45 p.m., when Heidstra reaches Dorothy Street via the alley, he turns left and heads back to his apartment. He walks past two or three houses before stopping again to look back towards Bundy. The dogs are still barking. Moments later, Heidstra sees a vehicle come out of the darkness on Dorothy near Nicole's condo. The vehicle is moving quickly. It stops at the intersection before turning south on Bundy.

"It appeared to be a wagon car, Jeep-like car," Heidstra testifies.

Although Heidstra will later admit to considering a book deal that never happens, Cochran gives him a chance to address the jury about his motivations.

Cochran: Are you here to favor either side in this case at all?

Heidstra: Not at all.

Cochran: Why are you here?

Heidstra: To tell the truth about what I saw and what I heard.

Cochran: Have you told us the truth here?

Heidstra: Yes, sir.

Heidstra's testimony is interesting to me as I consider Tom Lang. On several occasions, Heidstra tells both Cochran and Chris Darden that he meets with an LAPD detective, identified as Dennis Payne, on June 21, 1994. This is the same detective who interviews Tom Lang on June 20 – the same guy who Tom has doubts about.

Heidstra also testifies that, a few weeks later, Payne picks him up at home and takes him downtown to see Marcia Clark and Bill Hodgman. He says Hodgman asks most of the questions during the meeting while Marcia observes.

Cochran: Did Detective Payne say anything to you at that point?

Heidstra: No, he called me and said I was a crucial witness.

Just like Tom Lang, Heidstra expects to end up on the prosecution's witness list at some point.

Cochran: Were you ever subpoenaed to testify by the Prosecution at all?

Heidstra: Never.

Cochran: You were never subpoenaed at any time?

Heidstra: No.

Cochran: You are here today pursuant to subpoena from the defense aren't you?

Heidstra: Yes.

Instead of winding up on Marcia's witness list, it appears Heidstra soon finds himself on Darden's shit list. Heidstra testifies about a meeting with Darden and two other detectives on Memorial Day, 1995. They end up taking a walk around the block instead of squeezing into Heidstra's small apartment to talk.

Cochran: The conversation, can you describe for us the tone of the conversation between these three men as they asked you questions, specifically Mr. Darden?

Heidstra: Not very friendly.

When it is Darden's turn to cross-examine, the tone does not appear to get any friendlier.

Darden: Are you planning on making some money by testifying in this case, Mr. Heidstra?

Heidstra: Not at all.

Darden: Didn't you tell Patricia Baret when this case is finished you are going to make a lot of money?

Heidstra: I didn't say that.

Darden: You never told her that?

Heidstra: Maybe something might come out of it, but I never said a lot of money.

Darden: So you think you might make some money as a result of testifying in this case?

Heidstra: Maybe, I don't know.

Darden: And you could use a few dollars, right?

Heidstra: Yes, yes.

Outside the courtroom, Marcia Clark bad-mouths Heidstra — the same person her detective once called a "crucial witness."

". . . no one with half a brain would believe this guy," Clark tells reporters.

Apparently, Daniel Petrocelli, the lead plaintiff attorney in the 1996 civil trial, suffers from major brain deterioration based on Marcia's standards. Whom do the plaintiffs call as their key witness in the civil trial? Yes, that is right. Robert Heidstra. After Heidstra gives the same story of that night with little to no inconsistencies, Petrocelli, just like Darden, asks him about any plans to write a book. This line of questioning is a far cry from Darden's grilling a year earlier.

Petrocelli: Now, since that time, have you made plans to write a book about your observations?

Heidstra: Yes, after the verdict.

Petrocelli: Okay. Have you sold your book?

Heidstra: No. No takers.

Petrocelli: Nobody interested?

Heidstra: Guess not.

Petrocelli: You have not received any money at all?

Heidstra: Not all all, not one penny.

Simpson's attorney, Bob Baker, keeps his cross-examination short, sweet and mild during the civil trial. However, his very first question to Heidstra will serve as a memory refresher for all those in the courtroom.

Baker: When you were put on in the criminal trial, you were put on by Johnnie Cochran?

Heidstra: Yes.

Baker: Mr. Darden didn't put you on the stand?

Plaintiff attorney Michael Brewer successfully objects to the question as irrelevant, but the message is received.

In the criminal trial, Heidstra is one of the defense team's star witness. Bailey shares in his book that Patrick McKenna makes several drives from the crime scene to O.J.'s Rockingham estate to measure the amount of time elapsed. McKenna's best time is seven minutes. Bailey effectively subtracts that time from the moment Heidstra hears male voices.

". . . if Simpson was stabbing Ron Goldman at 10:40 p.m., that would have left him all of about eight minutes to dispose of his clothing and the weapon, shower away the blood residue, meticulously clean his shower, get dressed, pack, and appear at the front door at 10:55 p.m. with bags, ready to get into a limo, which had been parked outside his gates for 30 minutes without seeing anyone arrive."

Not so, says Petrocelli during the civil trial. His team times the drive at four minutes.

"Mr. Simpson probably got there faster that night,"

Petrocelli tells the jury during his closing argument.

Petrocelli subtracts those four minutes from 10:51, the time he says Kato Kaelin heard those thumps behind the guest house. He reminds the jury that Heidstra sees a white vehicle speed away from the area of Nicole's condo at about 10:45.

But what about all the other stuff Simpson has to do? Petrocelli offers an answer.

"And understand something. When Mr. Simpson left Bundy, this guy was in a hurry. He left all the evidence behind. He left his hat; he left his glove; he left his blood. He didn't clean up," Petrocelli says. ". . . He had time, later on, to dispose of evidence. He didn't have to dispose of the evidence between Bundy and Rockingham. He went from Bundy right to Rockingham and right upstairs, so he wouldn't miss that limousine."

I wonder what Marcia, and Darden for that matter, thinks of Petrocelli's closing argument and his use of Heidstra as a key witness. Obviously, Petrocelli is able to do what Marcia cannot – convince a jury of O.J. Simpson's guilt.

Again, 10:40 p.m. is not the time Marcia Clark says the murders take place. From the onset of the trial, Marcia sets the time of the murders at 10:15. In her mind, this gives O.J. ample opportunity during the time he is unaccounted for: between roughly 9:35 and 10:55 p.m.

"In between those two times, at 10:15, a dog is heard barking that the evidence will show was Nicole's dog, which fixes the time at which the murder occurred," says Marcia during her opening statement.

Marcia is referring to the very first witness *she* puts on the stand – Pablo Fenjves, who lives across the alley behind Nicole's condo. Fenjves tells the jury he is watching Channel

5 news at 10 p.m. in an upstairs bedroom with his wife.

"About 15-20 minutes into it, I heard a dog barking, sort of a plaintive wail."

Clark: Had dogs barked in that neighborhood before, sir?

Fenjves: Yes, but this was pretty persistent barking, it just wouldn't stop.

Petrocelli obviously is not there during the criminal trial to help Marcia along with her case. As a result, instead of embracing Heidstra's story, like Petrocelli did, and using it to her advantage, Marcia and Darden attempt to discredit one of the Dream Team's key witnesses. Pablo, not Heidstra, is their guy.

So what is Marcia Clark's issue with Tom Lang? He tells police that his brief encounter on the corner of Bundy and Dorothy takes place at 10:03. He is positive about this after retracing his steps dozens of times. Unlike Heidstra, his testimony seems to be a near perfect fit for Marcia's narrative. She can say that O.J. commits the murders 12 minutes after Tom and his dog walk by, and then O.J. has plenty of time to do the other stuff he needs to do before showing back up at Rockingham.

What is the problem?

The problem is – there is another timeline that often gets overlooked and is rarely discussed on the *bright* side of O.J.'s moon. A timeline that is even tighter than O.J.'s . . . a lot tighter. A timeline that leaves little to no wiggle room if you are buying what Marcia Clark is selling.

A timeline that can twist the whole murder case into different directions if you dare insert Tom Lang.

The timeline of Ron Goldman.

CHAPTER 17 – BAD TIMING

If you follow Marcia Clark's narrative, 38 minutes separate two important events in Ron Goldman's timeline on the night of June 12, 1994.

The first event is one that is undisputed and supported by phone records. At 9:37 p.m., Judith Brown, the mother of Nicole Brown, calls the Mezzaluna Restaurant. This is fact. The reason for Judith's call is to report missing eyeglasses after returning home from dinner at the restaurant that night. Nicole's family and friends had dinner at the Mezzaluna that night following her daughter's dance recital. O.J. was not invited.

The second event – the horrific murders of Ron and Nicole – happens sometime later. If you ask Marcia Clark, the murders take place 38 minutes after Judith's phone call at 10:15.

However, if you ask Daniel Petrocelli, who represents the victims in the civil trial a year later, the killings occur at 10:40. These are two people who are paid to make O.J. pay, in one form or another, and their stories are 25 minutes apart.

Tom Lang, the man who never gets a chance to share his story in either trial, is a problem for both.

We do know that Ron Goldman punched out on his time-card at 9:33 p.m. This is also undisputed. Karen Crawford, who mostly works as a bartender at Mezzaluna, serves as a manager on Sunday evenings and helps with the books. She testifies that she sees Ron walk over to punch out a few minutes before receiving Judith's phone call.

Clark: And did she ask you do something?

Crawford: She did.

Clark: And what was that?

Crawford: Umm, she asked me to look for a pair of glasses she had lost at the restaurant."

Clark: Okay. And what did you do?

Crawford: I looked around the restaurant and when I didn't find them out there, I remembered I had seen them coming in from outside, so I looked outside."

Remember, as Crawford looks inside and outside the restaurant, the stopwatch on Ron's timeline is already ticking. Crawford testifies that she eventually finds the glasses outside near the gutter, and then she gets back on the phone with Nicole's mom.

Clark: What did she tell you?

Crawford: She told me that she could not pick them up, she lived too far away, and that she would have her daughter pick them up.

Again, the clock is ticking, and Ron has not even entered the picture, yet.

Crawford hangs up the phone and puts the glasses in a white business-sized envelope. She writes *"Prescription glasses. Nicole Simpson will pick up Monday"* on the front, seals the envelope, and places it in the lost and found behind the bar. Tick. Tick. Tick.

Clark: Now, after you had that conversation with Mrs. Brown and you placed the envelope behind you at the bar, did you get another phone call?

Crawford: Yes.

Clark: About how long after the first phone call did you get the second phone call?

Crawford: About five minutes.

Clark: Okay, would you estimate then about 9:45?

Crawford: Yes.

Of course, with a roughly five-minute lapse between phone calls as Crawford suggests, that leaves only three minutes to speak to Nicole's mom (twice), look inside and out, and put the glasses in an envelope in lost and found, but let's go ahead and just stick with that time. 9:45 p.m.

In order to fit Marcia's narrative, Ron, who is sitting at a table talking to co-workers and enjoying a Pellegrino mineral water, now has 30 minutes to get to Nicole's condo when the murders take place. He is no longer wearing his tie and vest after punching out 12 minutes earlier, and he does not appear to be in a rush to get home. If he is in a rush, he would be home by now.

Crawford tells the jury that she recognizes the voice on the second phone call as belonging to Nicole.

Clark: Was it concerning the glasses?

Crawford: Yes.

Crawford testifies that Nicole asks to speak to Ron. She walks over and informs Ron that he has a phone call. She sees Ron speaking to Nicole, but has no idea what he is saying. More time off the clock.

Clark: Now, after he spoke for a while on the phone, what did he do?

Crawford: He hung around for a couple of minutes and then he asked me to give him the glasses, and I did.

According to her testimony, Ron also tells Crawford that he is going to drop the glasses off at Nicole's on his way to meet up with some friends at the Baja Cantina, a popular restaurant/bar in Marina Del Rey. She then watches Ron leave the restaurant through a side exit that goes out to Gorham Avenue.

Clark: Do you recall about what time it was?

Crawford: He left about 10 minutes to 10:00.

Crawford says she remembers the time as 9:50 because she makes a phone call to a video store to see if it closes at 10 p.m. Her friend is at the Mezzaluna at the time, and he wants to rent a video. Bartender Stewart Tanner, who plans to meet with Ron later that evening at the Baja Cantina, also testifies to him leaving at about 9:50.

Clark: Okay. And what was the last thing he said to you?

Tanner: He said he would talk to me later.

During the preliminary hearing of the criminal trial, John DeBello, general manager of Mezzaluna, tells Marcia Clark that Ron remains at the restaurant for about 15 minutes before leaving. Robert Shapiro reminds DeBello that he told the grand jury that it was "15 to 20 minutes."

If both Crawford and Tanner are accurate, Ron now has 25 minutes to get to Nicole's condo in time for the murders. Ron's timeline – the Marcia Clark version – is really getting squeezed now, and Marcia knows it.

Another undisputed fact in the case is that Ron now walks home to his second-level apartment at 11653 Gorham Ave. If you do a Google map search, the distance between this address and the former Mezzaluna address of 11750 San Vicente Blvd is .2 miles. Google even offers an approximate walking time of six minutes.

However, in order to take less time off the clock, Marcia relies on the testimony of Tia Gavin, another waiter working that night. Gavin, who actually serves Nicole's party of 10 that night, also lives on Gorham.

Clark: Now, from where you were living at the time, how long would it take you to walk to the Mezzaluna?

Gavin: Two minutes.

Clark: And then Ron Goldman, did he live closer to the Mezzaluna than you?

Gavin: Yes, he did.

Clark: And so how much closer was it?

Gavin: About a half a block closer, probably take him under two mintutes.

Clark uses this portion of Gavin's testimony in her closing argument.

"The other waitress in the restaurant, Tia Gavin, testified that it takes about a minute to walk from the Mezzaluna to his apartment," Clark tells the jury. "So even being a little generous, he got home by about 9:52, say."

Hogwash. According to Nike, it takes the average person about 20 minutes to walk a mile at a relaxed pace – and there is nothing in Marcia's narrative that suggests Ron is in a hurry. Tanner is still at work. Even walking at a Nike pace, Ron would cover 1/5 of a mile in about four minutes, and that does not include a busy intersection to start his trip.

Please do not take my word for it. Ask lead plaintiff attorney Daniel Petrocelli, who offers a more realistic walking time during his opening statement of the civil trial.

"It took Ron about five minutes to get to his apartment," Petrocelli tells a different jury about a year later.

If you believe Petrocelli, and you believe Ron's co-workers, Ron gets home no earlier than 9:55 p.m. I believe it is closer to 10 p.m.

What Ron does in his apartment after that, and how fast it takes him to do it, is anybody's guess. The only undisputed fact during this next segment of time is that Ron changes his clothes. Ron's sister, Kim, testifies that she finds his work clothes draped over his bedroom door. Marcia's story clock is still ticking. Twenty minutes remain.

"He changed, he freshened up, because we know he wasn't wearing that waiter's uniform when he was found, and so it would be reasonable to infer that he got to Nicole's house with the envelope sometime shortly after 10:00," Clark tells the jury.

Again, hogwash. In a span of two minutes of her closing argument, Marcia uses that phrase, "freshened up" four times. For many, this might imply that Ron does something less time-consuming than, let's say, a shower. Of course, Marcia has no idea if Ron showered or freshened up or whatever you want to call it after working a full shift as a waiter, but that does not stop her. She needs "freshened up" to stick. She is running out of time.

Again, Ron plans to meet with friends at the Baja Cantina in Marina Del Rey. Now, where I live in dusty, rural Arizona, a place called Baja Cantina conjures up images of a family-owned Mexican diner that sells fish tacos and cheap beer. In Marina Del Rey, it is something quite different.

I do a search of the Baja Cantina in Marina Del Rey, and it ends up on ww.complex.com in 2015 as one of the "Top 25 Douchiest Bars in Los Angeles."

"Baja is overrun with very pretty people with very little substance. You'll find men in tight t-shirts who have trickled down from Muscle Beach alongside actresses/models/singers who forgot to pursue their career because they were wasting their time at Baja on terrible margaritas and said men in tight t-shirts," the article states.

Based on this description, not to mention Ron's appearance on the game show, "Studs," I am going to lean towards shower. At least Petrocelli is honest with his jury about what he knows.

"Ron apparently did not shave, from the autopsy pictures that we will show," Petrocelli says. "We do not know if he showered."

During his cross examination of both Crawford and Tanner, Robert Shapiro hints at another activity that literally *eats* more time off the clock.

Shapiro: It's a small restaurant. Do you assume that if he sat down and ate with the manager that you would see it?

Tanner: Okay. Ummm he sat down with the manager after he was done with work. He didn't eat.

Interesting. What does Ron Goldman's autopsy report, which includes an examination of his gastrointestinal system, say?

"... Approximately 200 ml of partially digested semisolid food is found in the stomach with the presence of fragments of green leafy vegetable material compatible with spinach."

Did the health-conscious Ron Goldman make time to eat a spinach salad, weighing a little less than a half pound, while he was home? It does not appear he enjoyed a salad that night at the restaurant.

Shapiro: Did you see Mr. Goldman eat all that evening?

Crawford: No, I didn't.

So after he arrives home at no earlier than 9:55 p.m., it is very possible that Ron Goldman has showered and eaten a salad. Marcia's story is in trouble now, and he has not even started the drive over.

I use Google map to measure the driving distance between 11653 Gorham Ave. and 875 S. Bundy. It takes about three minutes to drive west about .6 miles, straight down Gorham before merging into Bundy.

Ron Goldman's timeline is really under siege for those who want to put him at the murder scene at 10:15 p.m. If he gets home no earlier than 9:55, he has 20 minutes available, and eight of those are used up with traveling – both walking and driving. Ron would have to be in a mad rush to complete his other tasks in such a small window of time, and that does not include other possibilities, like brushing his teeth, checking his phone messages, sifting through mail, watching the 10 o'clock news, or taking a dump.

If you think 10:15 is a problem for the prosecution, you should consider what happens when you throw Tom Lang into the mix. In his handwritten statement to authorities two days after the murders, he writes:

"ON SUNDAY EVENING AT 10 P.M. I LEFT MY HOUSE TO WALK MY DOG. . . "

When I interview Tom Lang in 2023, he insists that he sees his living room clock strike 10 p.m. as he walks out of the house with this dog, Zimba. He is also adamant that he reaches the corner of Bundy and Dorothy at about 10:03. I use Google maps again to measure the short walking distance between Tom's house at 975 South Bundy Drive, and Nicole's condo. Sure enough, the result is .1 mile with a walking distance of 3 minutes.

Where is Ron at 10:03 p.m.? He should just be getting back to his apartment, possibly munching down on a spinach salad, or "freshening up."

If you agree, that leaves the most important question of all. If Ron Goldman is still at home, who the heck is the man that Tom Lang observes on the sidewalk in front of Nicole's condo?

". . . I THEN ALSO HEADED WEST ON THE SIDEWALK ALONG DOROTHY TOWARD GRETNA GREEN BUT FIRST LOOKED NORTH – UP THE SIDEWALK ALONG BUNDY ABOUT 40-50 FT. UP WAS A MAN. (HE WAS AROUND MY SIZE 5'11, 175 – WHITE. HE HAD ON DARK CLOTHING. HE ALSO HAD A RIGID POSTURE WITH HIS FISTS CLENCHED . . . "

According to the autopsy report, Goldman weighed 171 pounds and "measured 69 inches from crown to sole" at the time of his death. Pretty close.

During my interview, when I ask Tom Lang to reflect about that man on the sidewalk with fists clenched, he has one answer.

"I think I saw Ron Goldman," Lang says. "I think he was there a lot earlier than people think. I think he left work a lot earlier than people think. He was there. I think maybe Nicole sent him away when OJ pulled up."

However, as much as I want to believe Tom, I also know the facts. Ron does not leave the restaurant any earlier than 9:50. Heck, we don't even have a phone call from Judith about the missing glasses until 9:37, and we know Ron went home first.

I keep thinking back to F. Lee Bailey's description of Tom as a witness. He ". . . may have been the only person who could have gotten a glimpse of the killer (or killers) that fateful evening."

Maybe F. Lee Bailey is right. If the murders take place at 10:15 as Marcia suggests, this mysterious man on the sidewalk has to be involved in some way, doesn't he? Again, Ron is still at home.

Then, something hits me as I am driving along Mohave Road in the Poston Valley to get to my school. Is there a way in which *both* Tom and Marcia are right? Is it possible? What about Daniel Petrocelli's time of 10:40. Where does that fit in?

I will soon offer a possible scenario in which the stars align for all three – Tom, Marcia and Daniel Petrocelli.

CHAPTER 18 – IF

One of the most bizarre storylines of this entire saga, on either side of O.J.'s moon, is a "hypothetical" confession eventually shared with the world in a highly controversial book and eventual television interview.

In November 2006, ReganBooks, an imprint of HarperCollins, announces a soon-to-be-released book titled "O.J. Simpson: If I Did It, Here's How It Happened." There are also plans to air a special television interview on Fox to help promote the book.

Even the title is enough to make a person's stomach turn, regardless if O.J. is the killer or not. If you did it? What the heck is that supposed to mean? O.J., please, let people grieve in peace. Just shut up and go play golf or something. Maybe you should spend your time thanking all your lucky stars that you are not rotting in a prison cell somewhere.

Needless to say, a huge public uproar soon follows. The families of Ron and Nicole are outraged at the publisher for allowing Simpson to capitalize financially on the murders, and nearly 60,000 people sign an on-line boycott of the book. Four days later, HarperCollins bows to the pressure and cancels both the book and the interview. Judith Regan, the head of ReganBooks, loses her job.

However, this story is just getting started.

First of all, it is not as if O.J. Simpson himself sits down and pens out a masterpiece confession for the ages. Instead, Regan hires Pablo Fenjves to interview Simpson and serve as the ghostwriter. Fenjves reportedly receives $150,000 for his services.

Does that name sound familiar? Yes, Fenjves also is a key witness for the prosecution in the 1995 criminal trial.

"To be given an opportunity to sit in a room with a man that I personally believe to be a murderer . . . it was hard not do it," Fenjves tells CBS News in 2007. "It was hard to pass on that project."

Fenjves claims that O.J., during one of several interviews, expresses anger that so many people never gave him a chance. O.J. then asks the ghostwriter for his opinion. Guilty or innocent.

"I said, I'm sorry O.J. I thought you were guilty then, and I still think you're guilty. He just exploded."

Fenjves adds that one of the first things O.J. says to him is that he has no plans to confess to anything.

"So I looked at him, and I looked at the attorney in the room, and I basically said, 'What am I doing here?'"

Fenjves says he then leaves the room and places a call to Regan on his cell phone. At first, the ghostwriter wants out.

"I said we should just pull out of this thing. This is all very squirrelly."

Squirrelly is one way to put it. Unethical or disgusting might be another. With Regan still on the line, Fenjves says he gives his cell phone to the attorney before continuing his conversation with O.J.

"He said, 'You know . . . I thought this whole thing was going to be fiction. I said, 'I don't know where you got that because I don't write fiction . . . I save the fiction for my screenplays."

If the book is not fiction, why do all parties involved agree to put "If" in the title? Could it have something to do with the money? A book like this stands to make a fortune for the publishers. Court documents later reveal that O.J. receives $1.1 million for his "hypothetical" stamp on the book and the interview.

O.J. leaves the room with the attorney, Fenjves says, and then returns a few hours later to apologize. Apparently, money talks.

"He said, 'I guess I'm nervous. I've been confused about this whole thing. Let's get started, and you know, do you mind starting with the easy stuff?'"

Fenjves says he agrees not to plunge into the night of the murders right away, but eventually begins to push O.J. for more details in order to "fashion some kind of intelligent narrative."

"At one point, he said, 'I'm not going to tell you I cut my wife's throat open and watched her eyes roll back in her head.'"

After the cancellation, the Goldman family, still owed the bulk of a $33.5 million settlement from the 1996 civil trial, successfully sue for the rights to the book. The family later changes the title to "If I Did It: Confessions of the Killer," and even adds some commentary of its own.

The original book is not the only thing cancelled in 2006. A television special to promote the book, featuring a taped interview with O.J., sinks right along with it. However, that interview, conducted by Regan herself, eventually resurfaces on March 18, 2018 as part of a special program on Fox called "O.J. Simpson: The Lost Confession?"

Twelve years later, one might expect a show like this to examine the Regan interview with some sort of objectivity. With Soledad O'Brien, an Emmy-award winning broadcast journalist, as its host, there is certainly hope, but that is where fair and balanced begins and ends.

O'Brien's panel of "experts" includes none other than Judith Regan, who once planned to make a boatload off the interview; Eve Shakti Chen, one of Nicole's closest friends who cannot stop crying during the entire show; Jim Clemente, a former FBI profiler out to prove Simpson's words bleed guilt; and Christopher Darden, the famed prosecutor who lost the biggest murder case in American history and is still stewing.

That is it. There is your panel.

No friends of O.J.

No defense lawyers from either trial.

No jurors from the criminal trial.

No media experts questioning Regan's motives at the time of the interview, or heaven forbid, challenging the credibility of paying someone to confess.

No representatives from HarperCollins to explain why they cancelled the book and later fired Regan.

No Pat McKenna.

No Tom Lang.

No O.J.

However, Fox is no dummy when it comes to ratings. The show hits the airwaves opposite a much-anticipated return of American Idol on ABC. Also, public interest in the case is still warm after an Emmy-award winning drama series, "The People v. O.J. Simpson," and an Oscar-winning documentary, "OJ: Made in America," appear two years earlier.

"O.J. Simpson: The Lost Confession?" The answer to this

question, in my humble opinion, is a resounding no. The program is a one-sided, obviously scripted, and admittedly hypothetical circus act with a sole purpose to make money. In the interview, O.J. reminds Regan and the world — over and over again — that his story is "purely hypothetical."

Regan blows a golden opportunity to bust Simpson on a variety of contradictions – much like attorney Daniel Petrocelli does in the civil trial. More importantly, she blows her chance to ask Simpson for some sort of proof of his guilt, and at least see how he responds. Doesn't every crime scene have specifics that only the killer and the police know about? It would be easy – especially easy if you have a man in front of you "confessing." Just ask him . . .

Where is the knife? You know (wink, wink), hypothetically, of course.

If it is me, I am asking about Tom Lang.

Were you parked in front of the condo on Bundy talking to Nicole a few minutes after 10? Did you see a man at the corner walking his dog?

Nope. Instead, Regan continuously refers to her book in order to guide O.J. along. There is no new evidence offered during the program. Instead, he repeats what is already in the book about a mysterious person named "Charlie" who is "hypothetically" with him on the night of June 12, 1994. Charlie "hypothetically" shows up at O.J.'s house to inform him about some shady stuff going on at Nicole's condo at that moment.

> *"I don't know why he had been by Nicole's house, but he told me you wouldn't believe what's been going on over there, and I remember thinking whatever is going on over there has got to stop."*

Without being asked by Regan to offer an approximate time, of course, O.J. talks about "hypothetically" driving over to Nicole's condo with Charlie.

"I'm kind of broad-stroking this," O.J. says.

No shit, O.J.

Regan is looking down in the book as he begins his story.

"Let's just go back and do the details. Where did you park?" Regan asks.

Responds Simpson, "In the hypothetical . . . in the alley."

"And you put on a wool cap and gloves . . . " says Regan, as she leads her witness.

'In the hypothetical," Simpson laughs, "I put on a cap and gloves."

O.J. says Charlie grabs a knife that he always keeps under his seat in case he runs into any "crazies."

"Charlie took the knife?" Regan asks.

"Yeah, in the book, yes." O.J. says.

Sometimes O.J. chuckles as he repeats these "hypothetical" details from the book. He puts off a vibe that he just wants to get the interview over with, collect his check, and go. After all, most people think he is guilty anyways. Maybe he thinks he has nothing to lose and $1.1 million to gain.

O.J. says he enters through the back gate, hypothetically, of course, and looks around. He sees candles lit inside the house. Music is on.

"While I was there, a guy shows up. . . a guy I really didn't recognize. I may have seen him around. I really didn't recognize him to be anyone, and in the mood I was in, I started having words with him."

Regan again refers to the book, in which Ron Goldman hypothetically informs O.J. that he is only there to drop off her mother's glasses.

"I don't know if I believed it or didn't believe it. It was pretty much immaterial, because I was more concerned about *everything* that was going on, and, uhh, I was fed up with it I guess."

That is when Charlie hypothetically follows "this guy" in with the knife.

"As things got heated, I just remember that Nicole fell . . . and hurt herself . . . and this guy kinda got into a karate thing. I said, uh, 'Well, you think you can kick my ass?'"

O.J. says the last thing he remembers is taking the knife from "Charlie." ". . . And to be honest, after that, I don't remember." Why? Because he blacks out.

He has never blacked out before June 12, and he has not blacked out since. When he comes to, he sees a bunch of stuff. What kind of stuff? Blood. Lots of blood. Regan gets O.J. to say he bundles up his bloody clothes, but she does not go any further on the topic, such as where he put them.

Regan does not ask O.J. for any more specifics from that night. She attempts to explain herself to O'Brien 12 years later.

"I don't know who Charlie is. I wanted him to talk," Regan says. "For me to start interrogating him and pushing him, I felt he would get more agitated, and he kept threatening to leave and not finish the interview, and I really wanted him to stay."

At one point, O'Brien turns to Darden for his take.

"Well. . . I think he has confessed to murder," Darden says. "If I had known he said this in 2006, I would not have objected to the release of this video. I don't think that there is any question of his involvement and that he is the person who is wielding the knife."

"I think Charlie is OJ. This is no hypothetical. This is reality."

As soon as Regan moves on to events that follow June 12, such as the big chase, and the big verdict, O.J. is quick to point out that he is no longer in a hypothetical mode. Even though he has just hypothetically told the world that he and an accomplice named Charlie are responsible for the deaths of Ron and Nicole, O.J. has a strong opinion about the Not Guilty verdict.

"I felt if that there is anything right in the universe, there is no way they convict me of this. And we're not talking hypotheticals here. That's how I felt."

Yes, O.J., that's how I felt, too. For a long time.

That is until one morning on my drive to work when I started thinking about my phone interview with Tom Lang. I truly believe he is a credible and honest witness with nothing personal to gain. I believe with all my heart that he is telling the truth about what he saw that night.

So, when it comes to the verdict, why am I on opposite ends with Tom Lang. He believes O.J. is guilty. He believes he saw Nicole standing by the curb near the white Ford. He believes he saw Ron Goldman standing on the sidewalk with clenched fists.

At 10:03 p.m.

But how is that possible? There just isn't enough time.

CHAPTER 19 – RON

This final chapter serves as my hypothesis for what happens that night, this time featuring Ron Goldman – not O.J. or Nicole – as the lead character. It is based solely on information gathered from books, phone calls and a computer in the Arizona desert nearly three decades after the fact.

It is June 12, 1994 in Brentwood, Calif. at the Mezzaluna, a cozy Italian diner that fits perfectly into the acute corner of a triangular intersection at San Vicente Boulevard and Gorham Avenue. Mezzaluna will never be the same after this night. Just three years later, after losing much of its local client base due to largely unwarranted negative publicity, owner Karim Souki closes the restaurant for good.

The Mezzaluna in Brentwood is one of four in a restaurant chain with others located in nearby Beverly Hills, as well as Aspen, Colo. and New York City. At this time, the Brentwood branch has a much better reputation than its sister in Beverly Hills. A year earlier, LA Times food critic Michelle Huneven blasts the Beverly Hills branch after waiting 40 minutes for her meal.

"The manager, when consulted on the matter, did not express the slightest concern or empathy," writes Huneven, who boxes her dinner to go that night. "... Clearly,

Mezzaluna has its share of customers — maybe too many. The management seems to be cultivating an indifference designed to discourage any more. We got the hint. We won't return."

On this night, however, all is good at the Mezzaluna in Brentwood on a slow, quiet and peaceful Sunday evening. It is almost closing time. The last few remaining patrons are mostly either heading for the door or waiting for their bill.

After a five-hour shift, 25-year-old Ron Goldman, the friendly, handsome waiter with a zest for life, clocks out at 9:33 p.m. He loosens his tie and removes his vest before treating himself to an ice-cold Pellegrino mineral water. He exchanges small talk with a few of his co-workers, including John DeBello, the general manager, who initials his time-card. DeBello is the man who hires Ron six months earlier after a former employee, Michael Nigg, puts in a good word.

While some of us might be looking forward to a soft bed this late after five hours on our feet, Ron Goldman is just getting started. The night is still young. He and Stewart Tanner, who is tending bar, finalize their plans to meet with some other friends at the popular Baja Cantina in Marina Del Rey later in the evening.

Make no mistake. There is a reason why Ron becomes a contestant on a dating game like "Studs" in 1992. On this syndicated TV show, two eligible bachelors each go on $100 dates with three women, and the eventual "King Stud" wins a fabulous second date of his choice with one of the women — all expenses paid.

As the episode reaches its not-so dramatic conclusion, host Mark DeCarlo asks Ron, the "tennis pro," where he would take his date, the beautiful Diane, if victorious.

"I figured we'd get a houseboat on the Colorado River for

a couple of days, and lie naked during the day, and make love naked at night."

Judging by some of the screams, the women in the audience are more than happy with his answer.

When I watched this episode for the first time a few years ago, I cannot help but wonder if Ron is talking about Lake Havasu for his dream date. It is where the Colorado River meets the Parker Dam, and it is one of America's favorite summer vacation destinations. At the time, it is common to see two-story houseboats here packed with bougie SoCal partygoers on a weekend binge of sex, drugs and alcohol.

Ron and I were born just 45 days apart. In my early 20s, I frequented Lake Havasu and the Colorado River as often I could with friends and family. I am an official "river rat." We always talked about renting a floating party barge of our own someday, but it never happened, of course. Now, I keep thinking to myself . . . maybe I bumped into Ron somewhere at my home away from home. Maybe he was standing in front of me at the drink line at Kokomo's, a very popular nightclub next to the London Bridge. Maybe we were in the same crowd enjoying an upside down beer at Sundance. Maybe we parked our boats close to each other at Copper Canyon.

Oh, those were the days.

Even though two of the three hotties select Ron as their preferred date, his competition, Anthony Paduano, a bartender, is the big winner after answering more questions correctly. Anthony and a young blonde woman named Val are off to Aspen where he wants to "melt the slopes during the day and snuggle by the fire at night." As the credits roll, Ron immediately walks over to Diane and embraces her with a deep kiss. Apparently, they had a nice first date because Diane is quick to oblige. Ron really is a stud – a sexy, charming, well-groomed stud now on his way to one of the No. 1 hotspots on Sunday nights.

At about 9:45 p.m., as Ron is about to leave, Karen Crawford, who serves as an assistant manager on Sunday evenings, informs Ron that he has a phone call waiting for him at the bar. It is Nicole Brown Simpson, who left Mezzaluna about 75 minutes earlier after having dinner with family and friends.

Ron and Nicole have been developing a friendship in recent months, and it is very possible that it was nothing more than just that – a friendship. Ron has many female friends at this time, and not all of them involve romance and/or sex. Earlier on this day, when another female friend needs help, Ron comes to her rescue, too.

As I read more deposition from the civil trial, one name catches my eye as an attorney asks Kim Goldman about certain people in Ron's electronic rolodex. It is Tracy LePera, who just happens to share the same last name as my elementary school. I find Tracy on social media, and she agrees to a phone interview. When I ask her if she might be related to Joseph LePera, our former principal and namesake, she says, "Yes, I am. He is my granddaddy's brother." Yet another crazy coincidence on this crazy journey.

Ron and Tracy are among a circle of close friends who live in the same small area of Brentwood, many of them residing in Tracy's apartment complex. Ron lives right around the corner in a different complex on Gorham Avenue, just a stone's throw away. They are all in their mid-20s — young and attractive. They call themselves "Brentwood Place," a tribute to Melrose Place, which is a popular prime-time soap opera on Fox about

20-somethings sharing the same Hollywood apartment complex. Less than a month earlier, 19.3 million people watch the Season 2 finale of Melrose Place. The title of this special two-hour episode? "'Til Death Do Us Part." Go figure.

"Brentwood Place" often gathers at Starbucks down the street for morning coffee. Tracy remembers meeting Nicole there for the first time.

"She would come in her Ferrari and sometimes Ron would be driving," Tracy says. "But they weren't together."

Sometimes, members of the group gather at the bar at Mezzaluna for a casual drink. However, their favorite passion is the LA club scene, where Tracy herself both works and plays. She is a promoter for some of the biggest clubs in LA, including China Club and Club Tatou. She meets the likes of Mick Fleetwood and Bruce Springsteen, and even dates Sylvester Stallone briefly.

"I just ran the list and decided who got in the club and who didn't, and dealt with celebrity seating and such," Tracy says.

Tracy will eventually marry and enjoy a successful career making big money in the corporate world. Today, she is divorced and enjoying a more simple life as a professional dog walker, but . . . back then?

"What can I say? I was a wild party girl," she says. "I ran the night clubs . . . dated some celebrities. It was a good time. I was gorgeous."

It is not uncommon, Tracy says, for alcohol and maybe a little bit of cocaine (there is that C word again) to make its way into the world of Brentwood Place. However, she says there is one member of their group who does not touch either.

"Ron didn't do drugs . . . didn't drink," Tracy says. "He was very healthy. He just loved to have fun, and he was a good friend."

A good enough friend that much earlier today, on June 12, 1994, Tracy calls Ron at home asking for help. She has locked herself out of her second-story apartment. Ron walks right over.

"He climbed up to the second-story balcony and broke into my apartment for me," Tracy says. "That is the kind of person he was. He was just a fun-loving guy . . . a driven, healthy young man."

In case you are wondering, yes, Tracy and Ron, too, are just friends.

"He wasn't really my type," Tracy says. "My roommate went out with him for just like two seconds, and that was it."

If Ron's friendship with Nicole *is* getting somewhat romantic, they are certainly keeping it to themselves. The close-knit crew at Brentwood Place does not even know about it. Nicole is obviously in a touchy situation with her ex-husband. Ron knows that and respects her privacy. Plus, Ron has a new girlfriend.

Which brings me back – way back — to the one single question that started this entire journey more than three years ago while folding some laundry.

How did Ron get to Nicole's house?

The question seems so inconsequential now compared to everything else I learn during this journey — Tom Lang, Michael Nigg, Pete Argyris, etc. etc. If I just read attorney Daniel Petrocelli's opening argument during the civil trial before I dive into Kim Goldman's deposition, I get an answer and this book never happens:

". . . After Ron changed, he got into his *girlfriend's car* parked in his garage, and drove the short distance to Nicole

Brown Simpson's home at 875 South Bundy Drive in Brentwood," Petrocelli tells the jury. "Ron parked the car on the side street, walked to the front of Nicole's condominium, and turned up the walkway to the front gate. . . "

Of course, the next obvious question is, who is Ron's girlfriend? I do not recall any references to a girlfriend in the media. Then I remember that very first day when I learn about Michael Nigg – by accident – while reading Kim Goldman's deposition. After Kim responds to questions about Michael, attorney Phillip Baker eventually asks her this:

> *Baker: And then he began to date Andrea Scott?*

> *Kim Goldman: In April or May.*

> *Baker: And they were still dating until his death in June?*

> *Kim Goldman: Yes.*

A quick internet search leads to me a 2017 documentary series called, "Is OJ Innocent? The Missing Evidence." The series examines a theory by private investigator Bill Dear, who is obsessed with a notion that O.J.'s son, Jason, is the real murderer. I prefer to stay away from this rabbit hole.

However, Episode 2 of this series features the first-ever interview with none other than Andrea Scott. The interviewer is Derrick Levasseur, who I immediately recognize from another one of my all-time favorite TV shows, "Big Brother." Derrick, who has an extensive background in law enforcement, is hands down the greatest contestant ever to compete in Big Brother, winning $500,000 in Season 16. Since then, he has enjoyed more success in the entertainment world as a true crime guru.

"This is a great opportunity for me to get an inside perspective on who Ron Goldman was as a person," Derrick says.

Andrea sounds much like Tracy when describing Ron. In fact, Tracy recalls meeting Andrea shortly before the murders take place.

"I've met her, and seen her, but it was very new," Tracy says.

During the interview with Levasseur, Andrea describes Ron as "full of kindness and happiness."

"He was a cool guy," Andrea says. "Always joking . . . very charismatic. A really good guy. Very good friend."

Derrick asks Andrea how Ron ends up with her car — a red Toyota sedan – on the night of the murders.

"Well, Ron was looking after my dog while I was out of town, and so because he didn't have a car, I said, please take my car."

Derrick and his co-host, Kris Mohandie, give special attention to Andrea's car keys found in Ron Goldman's hand at the crime scene. Andrea says an LAPD detective returns the keys to her in a sealed evidence bag about 3 or 4 days after the murders.

"He cut open the top and let me reach in and the keys were caked in blood. To wash it off, I had to physically rub it, it was awful."

This piece of information from Andrea suggests that LAPD never tests the keys for DNA. Bill Pavelic, the former LAPD detective turned private investigator for the Dream Team, describes Andrea's keys as the "mother of all evidence" in the O.J. Simpson case, "and the reason is it would either exonerate O.J., or it would absolutely implicate him."

It is difficult to gauge how serious Ron and Andrea are becoming at the time of the murders. In the book, "His Name is Ron," Andrea Scott goes to the Goldman family house after the funeral and returns a ring that Ron gave her. According to the book, the ring has three circles representing their first date, eventual engagement and wedding, but Andrea tells Kim that Ron "was only joking around."

Back to that night. When Nicole asks Ron if he can drop off her mother's glasses, Ron does not hesitate. He tells Nicole he will be there in about 10 minutes. A few minutes after hanging up with Nicole, Ron makes eye contact with Stewart Tanner at the bar as he walks towards the side exit. It is just before 9:55 p.m.

"I'll talk to you later," Ron tells Stewart.

Ron crosses the intersection at San Vicente Boulevard, and then Barrington Avenue, before continuing east on Gorham Avenue to his apartment complex. By this time, Ron already has a plan for helping Nicole, and it differs greatly from Marcia Clark's narrative. Ron has no intention of going to Nicole's *after* he gets ready. Instead, he is going over there . . . *before.*

Why? Even though Ron is definitely ready to party tonight, he appreciates that Nicole is certainly not. This is Sunday. It is late. Nicole is home alone with her children, and she has had a long, long day – the recital, the dinner, the arguments with O.J., the phone call from Faye Resnick less than an hour earlier that left her in tears. All of those have taken their emotional toll. While Ron does not get all these details over the phone, he understands that Nicole is exhausted. She has a nice relaxing bath ready to go as soon as Ron drops off the glasses and leaves.

Ron could walk to Nicole's from the restaurant if he wanted. It is a shorter distance. However, that means Ron would have to double back and walk all the way home. He knows this.

Just before 10 p.m., Ron arrives at his apartment complex at 11663 Gorham Avenue. Instead of going upstairs, Ron hops into Andrea's car and starts the engine.

I respectfully disagree, Ms. Clark and even you, Mr. Petrocelli. Ron does not change clothes first. Not this time. Still wearing his Mezzaluna uniform, Ron drives Andrea's car east on Gorham Avenue. This is why Ron is not inside his apartment taking a phone call. Instead, an unknown caller leaves a message on his answering machine.

". . . Ron, Ron, Ron, Ron, Ron, Ron, Ron, Ron. Hey bonehead, it's almost ten. I'm debating whether I'm just going to head over to your house or not. I want to get movin' here. I'll probably give it about ten . . . fifteen minutes. Call me. Later."

This phone message, which is shared on Page 1 of "His Name is Ron" by the Goldman family, is also a big reason why Marcia's Clark's narrative is bogus. He does not go home and "freshen up" at the speed of light as Marcia would have you believe. If Ron does that, he answers the phone call.

Ron drives east on Gorham before it merges with Bundy and turns south. Nicole's glasses are in a white envelope on the passenger seat. About eight minutes have passed since he walked out of Mezzaluna.

Almost immediately after the merge, Ron's headlights shine on a white Bronco parked along Bundy in front of Nicole's condo. The passenger door of the Bronco is open. Ron can see Nicole standing by the curb, talking to somebody inside the vehicle.

Ron parks directly behind the Bronco. Nicole is making this easy for him. He can just hop out, hand her the glasses, and be on his way. Another good deed accomplished. Piece of cake. His buddies are waiting.

However, there is a problem. As Ron approaches, he quickly realizes this is not a friendly conversation between Nicole and the driver of the Bronco. He hears a deep, angry voice from inside the vehicle.

"Who the fuck is that?!"

Nicole motions to Ron to stop. Ron, who is now standing directly in front of Nicole's condo, does just that. Ron knows about the ex-husband's violent history, so he is in stand-by mode. He is ready to pounce if the driver tries to get out of the vehicle and get physical with his friend. He clenches his fists.

Suddenly, as Nicole is still arguing with the driver, Ron notices a large dog approach from the opposite direction on Bundy. The dog has no leash. It is 10:03 p.m.

"Zimba, hup!"

Nicole watches the dog return to his master, a man she recognizes as a neighbor from down the street. Ron, who is more worried about who is inside the Bronco, makes brief eye contact with the dog walker before looking back at Nicole.

"This is not a good time, Ron," Nicole says. "I'm sorry."

Ron reluctantly walks back towards the car. He knows Nicole is upset, but she seems to have the situation under control.

"I'll come back in a little bit," Ron says in a soft voice loud enough for only Nicole to hear.

Without passing the Bronco, Ron backs up a bit and

makes a U-turn on Bundy. He puts the glasses back down on the passenger seat. At about 10:10 p.m., he arrives back at his apartment complex. Again, the night is still young.

Ron walks upstairs and enters his apartment. He immediately moves his way to the kitchen and opens the fridge. He is hungry. He throws some fresh spinach into a bowl and adds some low-calorie dressing. Another healthy dinner is served.

After he eats, Ron undresses and tosses his work uniform over the bedroom door before stepping into the shower. At the same time, the confrontation down the street between his friend and her ex-husband is intensifying.

Why? Because Nicole is finally done — really and truly done. She has reached that undeniable moment in a relationship when a woman, after going back to her abusive partner time and time again, has finally reached her point of no return. It is over. Nicole has expressed these words to him before, but the tone in her voice is different this time around. She is confident, defiant and unafraid. His responses, for the first time ever, mean nothing to her. They go in one ear and out the other.

O.J. has never witnessed this from Nicole before. He has completely lost control of Nicole, who is anxious to start a life on her own. The Hall of Famer in arguably the world's most violent sport knows only one recourse, and this time, he has a knife. It is 10:15 p.m. Pablo Fenjves, a neighbor across the alley behind Nicole's condo – the same man who will later ghost write O.J. Simpson's "hypothetical" confession, hears a dog barking from that direction.

Less than a mile away, in an apartment at 11663 Gorham Avenue, Ron Goldman is in the shower washing his hair.

Ron gets out of the shower and throws on some of his

go-out clothes. An autopsy report will later identify those clothes as Levi jeans, a long-sleeved shirt/sweater, and canvas-type boots over sweat socks. He brushes his teeth and sprinkles on something that smells nice.

At about 10:25 p.m., after he has brutally murdered the mother of his children, O.J. is still outside Nicole's condo, desperately trying to figure out his next move. By this time, the barking from Nicole's dog has subsided. O.J. starts to worry when he hears two people coming in his direction from the north. The conversation sounds casual, and the walkway into Nicole's condo is very dark. O.J. ducks out of sight, still holding the murder weapon, and remains silent.

Danny Mandell, who works in finance at Sony Pictures, and Ellen Aaronson, a production executive for the *Power Rangers* and other children's television shows, are walking back from their first and only date — at the Mezzaluna. They have agreed to take a longer route home to Ellen's apartment on Darlington Avenue so they have more time to chitchat. After exiting the restaurant, they walk west on Gorham Avenue on the north side of the street. As Gorham merges into Bundy Drive, they cross the street. This move puts them on the west side of Bundy going south.

As they will both later testify, Danny and Ellen do not see or hear anything unusual as they walk directly in front of Nicole's condo at 875 S. Bundy Drive. They have no idea a murderer covered in blood is lurking in the darkness just a few feet away. They continue south on Bundy, and just before they get to the front of Tom Lang's house, they cross Bundy again and continue walking east to Ellen's apartment on Darlington Avenue.

Tom Lang lives less than a minute away from Ellen at the northwest corner of Bundy and Darlington. When

Danny and Ellen get back to her apartment at 10:30, Tom has already returned home through his back entrance after walking Zimba around the block.

Meanwhile, Ron takes a bite of a Mrs. Fields cookie and sets it back down on the counter before putting on his watch and grabbing his wallet and keys. He walks by the answering machine without checking messages. His friends are waiting for him in Marina Del Rey, and he still has to drop off those glasses with Nicole.

Again, Ron takes the same route to Nicole's, west on Gorham Avenue until it bends south and merges into Bundy. This time, there is no white vehicle parked in front of Nicole's condo. The confrontation between Nicole and her ex-husband must have ended peacefully, Ron thinks to himself. He does not realize that O.J.'s Bronco is now parked in the back of the condo, or more importantly, that a murderer is still on the property.

Ron parks Andrea's car on Dorothy Street and walks to the front of Nicole's condo before entering the gate. Almost immediately, Ron sees Nicole's limp body near her front steps. A rush of fear takes over him. Before he can react, a large figure appears out of the darkness. O.J. Simpson, the man who once had everything in the palm of his hand – fame and fortune, an intensely beautiful wife, and an even more beautiful family, is now holding only a knife – a bloody knife.

Robert Heidstra, who is walking two small dogs in the alley behind the houses across the street, hears Ron's final words . . . "Hey, Hey, Hey!"

It is 10:40 p.m. on June 12, 1994. One of the top pop songs on the Billboard charts is "I'll Remember," by Madonna.

EPILOGUE

Just two days after I receive my manuscript back from the editor, and just when I assume all the bizarre coincidences are over, O.J. Simpson pulls a fast one. He dies.

On April 10, 2024 – 63 days short of the 30th anniversary of the murders – O.J. Simpson succumbs to prostate cancer in Las Vegas. The family announces his death through an official X account the following day.

The Goldman family responds with a statement, saying "the hope for true accountability has ended." I am not entirely certain what true accountability means for the family at this point, but it is clear the pain of losing Ron is still immense nearly three decades later.

"The news of Ron's killer passing away is a mixed bag of complicated emotions and reminds us that the journey through grief is not linear," they write.

Almost instantly, the bright side of O.J.'s moon, where discussion and debate over his guilt or innocence is forever constant, begins to illuminate just as bright as the days immediately following the murders. Maybe even brighter when you consider all the many different ways society is able to communicate today compared to back then.

Silly memes begin flowing throughout social media, such

as a photo of the slow-speed chase and a suggestion that O.J.'s funeral procession is conducted in the same manner. As I read all the social posts, something becomes very clear. The vast majority of people in the world accept that Ron and Nicole's killer is now dead, and they aren't pulling any punches.

> *"O.J. Simpson allowed to remain living after coffin doesn't fit."*

> *"A good bit would be the proctologist struggling to get the rubber glove to fit before the examination."*

> *"O.J. Simpson has died. In unrelated news, the killer of Ron Goldman and Nicole Brown Simpson has died."*

Or my personal favorite, O.J. dressed up as Prince in the courtroom, with a headline that reads,

> *"When Gloves Dry."*

Yes, the verdict of public opinion, which seemed at least a little bit up in the air for many years, is now a resounding *Guilty*.

As the news of O.J.'s death spreads, my close friends who I have shared this journey with often, are quick to come to me. One of my teachers asks, "So, are you mad you never got to talk to O.J.?"

The answer is not really. Unless he is going to confess, and I don't mean hypothetically, what would O.J. say to me that is new.

No. What angers me is that nobody gave Tom Lang a chance to talk to a jury about what he saw that night. I firmly believe that if he took the stand, and if he was able to look those jurors in the eyes and explain exactly what he saw, Mr. Simpson is sent to prison for the rest of his life.

Again, Tom has no motivation to lie. He never takes money. He never signs a book deal. Quite honestly, I am still surprised he let me interview him. He is a credible and convincing eyewitness who connects the dots for all of us who follow this case.

What angers me even more is that nobody really wants to talk about Michael Nigg . . . for Michael's sake. Not just because Michael serves as ammunition for insensitive and uninformed conspiracy theorists.

I am angry that police never talk to Stacy *immediately* after they arrest suspects for Michael's murder. The same goes for the five women enjoying a girl's night at the El Coyote Restaurant. Two of them get a good look at Michael's murderers. They could have given the district attorney what he needed to bring the suspects to trial, or they could have eliminated these suspects so investigators could focus in other directions.

Still, I always have to remind myself of something. If Ron and Nicole are still alive today, if the O.J. case and all the speculation that follows does not exist, if Stacy does not check on Michael's case after watching an O.J. documentary, if she never picks up the phone and calls LAPD Detective Scott Masterson, the unsolved murder of Michael Nigg is still sitting on a shelf in the LAPD archives collecting dust.

I return from my journey to the other side of O.J.'s Moon with one hope – that somebody will go back there. Soon. Somebody who has a much better spaceship than I do.

I believe there are many more craters out there to explore. I believe there is more to the story of Pete and JoAnn Argyris, including a strong chance that somebody *else* was involved on the night that led to the death of Brandon Davis. I suspect there is a small crater on the other side with that person's name at the bottom.

Michael's cowardly killers are hiding over there, too, inside a deep, dark crater. However, I know there are many private eyes, investigative journalists, web sleuths, social media influencers and other crime buffs out there with lunar landers much more advanced and equipped than my own. I believe they have the skills and resources needed to flip O.J.'s moon around, shed light on Michael's case, and bring his killers to justice.

Keep going.

ABOUT THE AUTHOR

B.T. "Weed" Wedemeyer is an elementary school principal in rural Arizona more than 15 years removed from a successful career as a newspaper reporter and editor. Before that, he served in Operation Desert Storm as a photojournalist for the United States Air Force. Today, the 55-year-old is an active volunteer in his community, a loving husband and proud father.

In 2021, as he casually watched a documentary about the most talked-about murder case in American history, Wedemeyer had a simple question about the case and entered it into an Internet search engine. When he didn't get his answer right away as he expected, the former news hound started digging and making phone calls. He returns more than three years later with some incredible true stories with both direct and indirect links to the O.J. Simpson murder trial.

This is his first book.

11975464R00125